CLOSER

CLOSER

DENNIS COOPER

Grove Press
New York

Grove Press
841 Broadway
New York, NY 10003

Published in Canada by General Publishing Company, Ltd.

The section entitled "GEORGE: Wednesday, Thursday, Friday" has previously
appeared in the anthology *Between C & D: New Writing from the Lower East Side
Fiction Magazine* (Viking/Penguin Books, 1988). The section entitled "CLIFF:
The Outsiders" has previously appeared in the anthology *Men on Men: Best New
Gay Fiction* (New American Library, 1986). Excerpts from *Closer* have appeared
in the magazines *Between C & D*, *Cuz* (New York City), *Farm* (Chicago),
Forehead (Los Angeles) and *Out/Look* (San Francisco). The epigraph by Robert
Pinget is from his novel *Mahu, or the Material*, translated into English by Alan
Sheridan-Smith (London: John Calder Editions, 1967).

I'm very grateful to Walt Bode, Christopher Cox, Raymond Foye, Amy Gerstler,
Felice Picano and Ira Silverberg.

This is a work of fiction. Any resemblance to actual events or locales or persons,
living or dead, is purely coincidental.

Library of Congress Cataloging-in-Publication Data

Cooper, Dennis, 1953–
    Closer/Dennis Cooper.—1st ed.
        p.   cm.
    ISBN 0-8021-1093-2
    ISBN 0-8021-3212-X(pa.)
    I. Title.
    PS3553.O582C56   1989
813'.54—dc19   88-27396
                                                          CIP

Designed by Irving Perkins Associates

Manufactured in the United States of America

First Edition 1989

First Evergreen Edition 1990

for Richard

CONTENTS

JOHN: THE BEGINNER   3

DAVID: INSIDE OUT   21

GEORGE: THURSDAY, FRIDAY, SATURDAY   39

CLIFF: THE OUTSIDERS   53

ALEX: THE REPLACEMENTS   69

GEORGE: WEDNESDAY, THURSDAY, FRIDAY   87

PHILIPPE: MAKE BELIEVE   101

STEVE: THE FOREFRONT   113

When you're expecting bad news you have to be prepared for it a long time ahead so that when the telegram comes you can already pronounce the syllables in your mouth before opening it.

—ROBERT PINGET

CLOSER

JOHN

THE BEGINNER

John, 18, hated his face. If his nose were smaller, his eyes a different brown, his bottom lip pouty . . . As a kid he'd been punched in the mouth and looked great for a couple of weeks. Six years ago punk rock had focused his life. John liked the way punk romanticized death, and its fashions made pretty good camouflage. He dyed his hair blue-black, wore torn T-shirts, smeared his eyes with mascara, and stared at the floors of his school like they were movie screens. He'd never felt more comfortable with himself.

Nowadays punk bored his schoolmates. John stuck it out, but the taunts and cold shoulders were threatening to ruin his new confidence. One afternoon he hitchhiked home, grabbed a pencil and paper and wrote down his options. "Make enemies." Trouble was, he'd always felt so indifferent toward people. "Therapy." That might have meant he was hopeless. "Art." On the strength of some doodles he'd done as a kid, and that his mother had raved about, he enrolled in a life drawing class.

John's teacher was fairly impressed. He announced to the class that the "work" was "unique" and compared it to "brilliant police sketches." John knew this was only a guess but the attention was just what he needed, so he refused to confirm or deny any interpretation, no matter how stupid. It was the tactic his favorite bands had always used to stay hip. That did the trick. Students would crowd around him after school and kind of hint how they wouldn't mind modeling when he had a moment.

He didn't have time to draw everyone, but being picky meant choosing an artistic goal. John couldn't. He didn't know what he was doing. He wound up selecting the best-looking students because they were fun to deface, and pretty easy to bullshit. He'd just sort of casually say that maybe he was portraying how tortured they were behind their looks and they'd gasp at his scribbles like they were seeing God or a UFO.

One afternoon a sophomore named George Miles took a seat in John's bedroom and tried not to blink. He'd looked cute, maybe even a little too cute, across the school cafeteria but one-on-one he twitched and trembled so much he made John think of a badly tuned hologram. John tried to draw but George was already ruined without his help. "I'll take a Polaroid," he thought, "in case I become a photographer." Reaching for the camera, he happened to notice the bed. No film. "Listen, I've got another idea," he said.

In bed George shut his eyes, went limp, and kind of

squeaked, all of which were okay with John. He'd only had sex a couple of times, once standing up in a toilet stall, the other time with a guy about fifty who'd done all the work while he held his ass open. With George as a prop, he tried out a bunch of positions he'd seen in a porno film. He made a lot of mistakes, like it took him forever to get his cock hard enough to slip inside George's ass, but if George noticed or cared, it didn't show.

The next morning John's drawing teacher asked him to stay after class for a few minutes, waited until the room cleared, then announced that although John "quite rightfully" liked to let his "heavy artistry" speak for itself, he might use the platform of an upcoming assembly to "help enlighten . . ." John tensed up. "No way," he thought. "In the words of the rock star Bob Dylan," the teacher concluded, eyeing John's clothes, "why not 'shovel a glimpse into the ditch of what each one means.' It'll count as a test."

From being a punk, John felt a slight pang of conscience. Punk's bluntness had edited tons of pretentious shit out of American culture, so, although John suspected that his work was nine-tenths pretentious shit, he tried to take the quote seriously, despite its has-been author. He agreed to the lecture idea, then spent a month taking notes and rewriting the notes until they didn't embarrass him. At dawn the day of the assembly he chewed on a pencil and tried to read what he'd written.

"Punk orders us to demystify everything in the world or we'll be doomed to a future so decadent, atomic bombs will seem just one more aftershave lotion and so on. What you seem to like in my drawings is how they reveal the dark underside, or whatever it's called, of people you wouldn't think were particularly screwed up. But you should know the real goal of my work is a Dorian Gray type of thing. I make you look awful, and I start to look really good. . . ."

That afternoon he stood in front of the dimmed student body while slides of his portraits appeared on a giant screen over his head. He was planning to speak after thirteen or so. As he studied the mostly bored audience, he couldn't help but distinguish a few guys he'd drawn or still intended to draw scattered through the forgettables. He reread his speech, thought it sounded too much like he didn't know what he was saying, grabbed the microphone and blurted, "My portraits speak for themselves."

Afterward most of the teachers avoided him. Five students put out their hands. He scheduled a couple of sittings, then chucked his script into a wastebasket. He smoked a joint and was wondering what his work might actually say if, through some sort of miracle, its lips could move, when he stumbled on George vomiting in a rest room. "How did you like my talk?" John asked. "I didn't go," George replied, looking down at the mess he'd made. "I don't want to know what your work is about."

John drew a circle. He added two vertical lines, spaced several inches apart, to make a neck. Facial features appeared on the page as random shaky lines, fine as the hairs on a barbershop floor. They became lifelike through shading. That involved tilting the pencil then dragging it along the grain of the paper in various directions. Two sloppy ovals came next. John filled them with black blobby shapes that were meant to be pupils but could have been something he'd spilled on the page accidentally.

John studied the portrait, then George's face, then the portrait, and made the eyes look like caves. It looked more like an ad for some charity. He tried to erase the eyes. The paper tore. He threw the sketchpad aside. "George," he groaned, "let's get undressed." They lay on the bed and put their faces in each other's crotches. At one point John leaned back and made absolutely sure George was as cute as he'd thought a few minutes before, then he plunged in again.

He felt something that could have been love but was too manageable and kind of coldly interesting. It was more like he understood how love might feel. The sensation itself wasn't anywhere as disorienting as love was rumored to be. Actually it didn't feel that different from having completed a portrait, except George's skin felt so great. That was the weirdest part, feeling how warm and familiar George was and at the same time realizing the kid was just skin wrapped around some grotesque-looking stuff.

"Huh?" That was George's voice. John was about to say, "I didn't say anything," when come spurted into his mouth. "Jesus, George," he choked, "couldn't you warn me or something? I was figuring something important out. Shit." To keep from causing a scene he turned his back and sulked. Propped up against the far wall was the portrait of George side by side with a sketch of a previous subject. Even damaged, George's looked better. John scrambled out of bed, grabbed his sketchpad and started comparing the portrait with every other one he'd finished. "Hey," he muttered, "I've got an idea. Get dressed."

They headed for Dump, a poorly lit gay bar well known for its loose clientele. John dropped George off on a barstool, then felt his way along the walls, squinting. After a few rounds John spotted someone he liked slouched on a gray vinyl couch near the video games. The guy wore his hair in a shark fin straight down the top of his head. It looked as stiff as a saw. His eyes were outlined with mascara. His mouth dangled open. The button he'd pinned to his torn leather jacket read, *I have many brains but I can't think.*

John ordered George to sit down at one end of the couch, and took his place at the other. The punk tried to seem unimpressed by their cruising, but eventually he turned and glared at the worse offender. It took him an hour to stop calling John a fake punk, faggot, scum, asshole. . . . George fell asleep. John feigned boredom until the punk started to nod out. Then he mentioned the drugs he had stashed in his bedroom. "Sounds good," the punk yawned. They made it home. After a few joints he said John could watch him jerk off.

John had the punk and George lie side by side on the bed. He crawled over their bodies while they masturbated, examining each in great detail and making comparisons. Below the neck they were just about even: smooth, washed-out, skeletal. Face-wise the punk wasn't much. His eyes were drab, his nose had been broken, his ears were caked with wax, his skull was shaped like an egg. He would have been nothing without punk. John sympathized at first. Then he realized he'd better not care or he'd never get hard enough.

He rolled George onto his stomach then climbed on top, tried to get his cock hard, couldn't, thought he could stuff it up George with his fingers but that didn't work so he rolled George back over and fucked his mouth. The punk sat a few feet off, watching them with a vacant expression that could have meant anything. John tried not to care but it attracted his eyes like a mirror. When he finally managed to come his concentration was so bad he missed George and got sperm all over everything. "Shit."

A few blocks away from John's parents' place there was a cobwebbed mansion that two generations of neighborhood kids had dubbed "the haunted house." It sat far back from the street.

To reach it kids had to scale a brick wall, then wade through an acre of dried grass and faded newspapers. Until he was twelve, John was too overwhelmed by the words "haunted house" to check the place out. When he finally tiptoed inside one afternoon it was nothing, an empty thing. He'd spent a half hour picking up pieces of broken chairs, used prophylactics and smelly bums' clothing.

The morning after the three-way with George and the punk, John woke up from a nightmare in which that house happened to figure. "Hmm." He roused the boys, then suggested a field trip. The punk shrugged, staggered down the hall, came back with a can of John's mother's hairspray and started repairing his mohawk. George crawled out of bed. He was moving a little mechanically, as if afraid he would drop something. "So, did you sleep?" John asked. "Bad dreams," George squeaked, then shook his head back and forth to erase the word. "Actually, uh, well, last night was the first time I realized . . . Oh, forget it."

As soon as they'd scaled the wall, John and George fucked in some bushes. The punk watched for a while, then he kicked them until they quit. All three collapsed on the steps of the house, dusty and spent as ghosts. John tried to tell them the story of how he'd discovered the place, but after a few minutes George strolled inside and started tapping the walls for possible secret compartments. The punk seemed more interested in the graffiti left over from earlier trespassers. He ran around scrawling the best on the backs of his hands with the tip of a burnt wooden match.

John ended up at a second-floor window, half listening to their racket. He watched a blond about eight years old ride his bike past the front of the grounds very fast. John imagined how frightened the kid would have been if he'd glanced up and spotted a male silhouette. Or had the world gotten so generally

ugly and fucked up since he was a kid that a haunted house
seemed kind of quaint? "If that's true," he thought aloud, "then
so are my drawings. God, I can't think about this." He called the
punk and George. The second they entered the room he ordered
them to strip.

The punk punched a hole in the wall instead. George bit his
nails. After glancing from John to the bloody fist about a dozen
times he stumbled into the hall. John rolled his eyes, crossed his
arms and tried to look like he meant what he'd said. The punk
punched another hole, then another, then another, et cetera.
John was deciding to leave when the punk paused, checked out
the holes, which formed a crude five- or six-foot-square
swastika, grinned for the first time that John could remember,
and started hitting himself in the face and chest.

His belt rattled. It was a handful of bicycle chains twisted
together and held in place with a rusty combination lock. Once
in a while he'd quit hitting himself long enough to spin the dial a
few times, squint, yell out some numbers, try the lock again,
swear, and go back to hitting himself. John was mesmerized,
the way he was when he did lots of weird combinations of drugs
and felt like he could control other guys with his mind. In this
case the cuts, bruises, scabs and blood smears made the punk
look a bit like John's portraits.

The punk got his belt off, stripped naked, and threw himself
onto a mattress that someone had left in one corner years back.
"Hurt me," he yelled in a hoarse voice. "Fuck me up and I'll
never forget you. I really fucking love violence. I want to tell all
my friends what we did so they'll hate me or call me a fag or
whatever, but fuck them. I'm not a poser like they are. I want to
do everything so when I die they'll say I lived and tell bad jokes
about me but who cares. I like getting crazy and you seem okay.
Anyway, why not?"

John thought, "If my drawings could talk I bet they'd say

something like that." "Okay," he said. He rolled up his sleeves and knelt over the punk's heaving back, fanning the B.O. away from his nose. He took a deep breath, then sank his teeth into the curve of one shoulder. "Leave a mark," the punk whispered. "Leave marks wherever you want. Make it memorable or whatever." This time John bit very hard. The skin still wouldn't break. "Try the back of my neck."

When John withdrew he saw some holes in the shape of an Xmas tree ornament. "That's it," he said. "I've got an idea. Get ready." The punk balled his fists. John bobbed his way down the back leaving bites in a regular pattern, four across, every few inches. Reaching the ass-slope he paused, massaged his sore jaw. The wounds were a really crass pink except the ones farther up, which had turned kind of violet. A few even leaked blood in long, thin strands that reminded him vaguely of tinsel.

He leaned back a few inches, spooked by the power of what he was doing. He tried to remember the name of the famous artist who'd shot himself and crawled across broken glass in his Jockey shorts. He couldn't. This seemed more original anyway. Doing horrible things to yourself was just me-generation angst shit from the seventies. A bleeding punk kid was so much more horrific and ridiculous and sort of moving too. Was that because of the Xmas connection? He thought suddenly of the pile of chains, smirked. "I'll make his ass a gift."

He pushed the punk's legs apart and adjusted them like an old TV antenna until the ass was roughly the shape of a box. Then he picked up the chains. Each lash left a red ribbon. He tried to aim, but the ribbons still came out too lopsided, so he had to make the whole area red. He was filling it in when the punk got impatient, rose up on his elbows and craned his neck to get a preview. First his eyes froze on something behind John. "It's the cops," he croaked.

It was George framed in the doorway, one hand clamped over

his mouth. "Don't move," John said. George took off. John chased him downstairs and out the front door. Midway across the yard John grabbed George's shoulder, ripped a hole in the shirtsleeve and brought them both crashing down on a pile of old newspapers. "I want . . . you to know . . . that had nothing to do . . . with us," he puffed. George struggled up to his feet, clutched his left knee and winced. He managed to say, "But I thought . . . ," then he hobbled away.

John wandered back to the room. It was empty. On the wall next to the mattress he found a fresh swatch of graffiti. *Bill was here more or less.* A trail of blood led from there to the door. John followed it down the hall. At its end he could just see the punk's silhouette shivering in the light coming through a smashed window. John accidentally stepped on a creaky board. The silhouette tensed, turned, broke a chunk of glass off what was left of the pane and held it out to John like broken glass was a gift.

"Kill me," the silhouette rasped. "I can't feel anything. I mean you're okay. Shit, I don't know. . . . I guess I've wanted somebody to kill me for over a year or whatever so don't fucking worry. Do what you want to me. I don't care. Really. When I'm dead you can fuck me as much as you want. I've tried to kill myself lots of times. I just can't. Anyway, nobody knows I'm here. You won't get caught—" "Stop," John said, waving his arms, "wait, I feel . . ." He vomited down the front of his shirt.

John bought the latest issue of *Art News,* hitchhiked home and flung himself on his bed. He surveyed the pictures, read a few scattered reviews. The only name he recognized was Carl Andre's because of a slightly embarrassing scene at the city museum three months before. John had entered its modern wing, seen a bunch of metallic squares on the floor, and asked the guard when the installation would be finished. He'd been brusquely informed that "the floor" was this man's work of art.

Maybe if it had been some kind of punk anti-art thing he would have thought it was great. But a critic was talking about "classicism." "No way." John skipped a few dozen pages. He preferred advertisements to articles anyway. With them he could draw *his* conclusions. Take the puke-colored painting of some young boy's head in the ad he was squinting at. "This artist hated his childhood so much," John mused, "it makes him vomit." He gasped when he noticed the work's title, *Jonah and the Whale,* in the small print.

He'd guessed right. It was the first time that he could recall being right about art and this shook him a little. Sure, it could have been some kind of fluke, but if it wasn't and he was beginning to understand art, that might mean he could understand what he was trying to do with his life. What if that ruined his work? What if his drawings weren't really important at all except as places to put his confusion, and once he'd figured that out, the inspiration for them would dry up like the wife-and-kids fantasies he used to have as a kid?

John noticed the word YOU in block letters so large and blue it could have been a kind of summons from God. It was only an ad for the School of New American Art offering critiques to young artists who sent in samples of their work, fifty bucks, and an s.a.s.e. John stared at the word for a while then decided he might as well mail in some stuff and let the experts tell him what he ought to do next. He grabbed the sheaf of his drawings, took out several of George, snuck into his parents' bedroom and stole some cash from the drawer where they kept their emergency funds.

The following month's only highlight occurred on a Thursday.

John had been keeping his eye on one particular freshman all year. The guy had a cherubic face. It was meticulous, as though conceived by computer, but in every other way he was a shambles. He talked out loud to himself, walked around in what seemed like a hypnotic trance, claimed that he was a pop star, et cetera. David always had the unnerving effect that George usually did during sex, or that that punk had had when John was biting him up. But pending word from the experts, John tried to avoid being overly ambitious.

That day they happened to stand side by side at the same urinal. John was so agitated he couldn't start to piss. Even from inches away, David was one of those guys who were so cute their skin looked like plastic or candy. He was oblivious to John and spent their precious few seconds together babbling to the wall behind the urinal about how somebody was following him. It was all John could do not to interrupt, not that he'd know what to say. He couldn't decide if he wanted to draw David, fuck him, beat him up or fall in love with him.

On the way home from school John took a detour so he could walk through a park. The usual ghosts of themselves were throwing balls in slow motion down corridors marked on the lawn. Balls stopped wherever. The old guys cheered in their rickety voices. Using his books as a pillow he lay on his back and watched the clouds move around for a while. He was glad no one he knew was nearby since he had to admit he found the sky kind of peaceful, despite the clichés that had piled up there over the centuries.

He let his mind veer all over the place. The sensation was sort of like being chased through the dark by a mob, or trying to chase down a mob that had split off in different directions. He closed his eyes and maybe half fell asleep, he wasn't sure. When he reopened them he'd forgotten what he had been dreaming. It was dark. He picked himself up. At the edge of the park he took a piss on the feet of a statue of some long-forgotten war hero, a granite man covered with bird shit.

That night he was drawing a boy named Simon whose head was shaped like a large glass of milk with some brown turf on top, chalky eyes and the mouth of a fish. Maybe it was John's nap but he couldn't get into the session. They shared a joint, then a beer, still nothing. John saw Simon to the front door making various excuses, none of which made any sense. They were waving goodbye when his mother strolled up with a letter for John in her hand. "And clean your room," she said.

The letter was one typed page, single-spaced. A Professor James somebody liked John's submission. He said some stuff that John didn't quite get about "straddling a line between confusion and hard-edged realism," and "passive-aggressive pencil work," and how the drawings were "obvious mirror images of the artist," and general words of encouragement. John ran to the phone, dialed George's number then hung up. "What the fuck am I thinking?" he thought. Instead he ran into his room, shut the door, turned the lock and yelled, "Great!"

One month and fourteen tries later John had George down. He glanced from portrait to model and back a few times, ripped the page from his sketchpad and held it at arm's length for George to see. "I think I look like I'm wearing a Halloween mask," he whispered. "That's true," John laughed. "Oh, wait, you mean in the drawing." He double-checked. No, George was too stoned or something. The sketch was an obvious masterpiece in every possible way. John hadn't felt so spooked by anything or anyone since he'd noticed that haunted house when he was five or six.

He stripped and walked into the bathroom. The stress of completing the portrait had left him unusually raunchy. He ran a damp washcloth under both arms, across his cock, between the cheeks of his ass. He tried to whistle the tune of The Smiths' "Handsome Devil" but the thing had no melody so he just sounded asthmatic. He smelled the rag and threw it over the top of the mottled glass door of his shower stall. When he got back to the bedroom George automatically stripped, and lay face-down on the bed.

A week later they went through the motions again. George sat on the chair near the window and got that weird look on his face that John decided meant one of two things, "Don't hurt me," or "What's the matter?" John could vaguely remember when George had meant danger. Now he was only the easiest guy to lay hands on. There was nothing intimidating about him at all. Nothing. John put down his pencil and pad. "George," he said, "something is obviously bothering you. Not just today but in general. So what is it?"

George's head jerked. "Oh, umm . . ." His eyes flicked all over the room. "Everything," he mumbled. John asked again then wished he hadn't because George's head gave a last shake or two and dropped back on the chair like he'd been shot. "I'm just completely fucked up," he whispered. "I don't have any real friends and I can't do my homework at all anymore. Sometimes I wish I was dead. Nothing makes sense like my mother has cancer and I don't know what's going to happen to me when she dies. It's nice to see you but I'm so alone all the time. . . ."

George went on like that for an hour, despite having made every point he was going to make in the first thirty seconds. John managed to seem like he cared because the fact that George had any troubles at all was so unexpected. The actual troubles were serious, John supposed, but there was nothing profound about them. Maybe they were a little more nerve-wracking than other pretty young men's, maybe not. John could hardly be sure, since he'd never been handsome himself.

Later they fucked or, rather, John fucked George and kept his eye on the last and definitive portrait, which, luckily, he'd framed and hung in clear sight of the bed. He put George through their usual twists and occupied himself trying to phrase the announcement he knew it was time to make. Words didn't seem that appropriate until they'd dressed, reached the front door and promised to phone. "I hope you understand," John added suddenly, "that I'm a much better artist than I am a person."

"I don't know what you mean," George said. He rested his hand on the doorknob. "I mean I've decided to make art my life," John said, "and if I'm going to do that I can't let myself deal with why you're fucked up. My work's my mirror, like that professor said. I'm weird enough as it is without figuring out why I'm so weird, if you know what I mean." George nodded, turned the knob. "You mean I scare you?" he asked. "No, I mean I can't see you again." George started trembling. "Oh."

John put George out of his mind, which wasn't easy since the guy's face was all over his work. One day he stuffed his drawings away in a bureau and canceled upcoming appointments. School closed for Xmas. He spent the holidays drinking himself sick in nightclubs. One of the packages under the tree was a blank book. He described his activities in it. When classes resumed he enrolled in creative writing, having reread his entries a few times and mused, "Genius."

Unlike John's life drawing teacher, the writing teacher kept up with cultural shifts. Mr. McGough didn't strain to include dated slang in his talks. He was forty-six but claimed his life had been changed by "that bump in the road to salvation called punk."

Jules remembered John's lecture and spent a few minutes one class discussing how clever John's statement had been. John shrugged and let Jules believe he'd calculated the outburst. After that Jules seemed to look upon him as an equal. They hung out a lot.

John guessed Jules was gay. He'd do things like one night he asked John to name every rock singer he'd like to draw and/or fuck. After a few dozen, Jules raised one hand and pinched the bridge of his nose like a psychic. "Your ideal," he said, "is a pale brunet, your age, thin, male, sad eyes, big lips. His nose is perky. His ears might as well be invisible they're so attuned to his face, like the handles on something one lifts to one's mouth when thirsty. . . ."

Jules talked like that because he was a poet. One of his best poems included this image: "a boy's screaming countenance faced the horizon, emitting a fresh brand of sunlight." Vaguely inspired, John hitchhiked home the day he read it and made a drawing. Jules liked that. Next thing John knew they'd begun a collaborative project in pictures and words. Jules arranged, with John's punk roots in mind, to hang their work in the janitor's closet, which, as it turned out, was much roomier than John had thought.

Sometimes when Jules finished a poem John would stay up all night adding smudges and smears to an earlier drawing until the two seemed to relate. Other nights he'd erase part of a portrait and give Jules free use of that space. By sticking to George, John not only recycled old stuff, he gave the newer work continuity. It took several weeks to complete the allotted thirteen. One evening John laid them out on Jules's living room rug. They clunked their beer cans together. "When this is all over," Jules announced, "let's have a three-way with some jerk."

They held their premiere during lunch hour. Most of the

faculty drifted through, eyeing the work with suspicious expressions. Among the students who came was a very drugged George. He took two wobbly steps into the room, tried to focus his eyes and groped around for the nearest wall. Jules studied George for a minute or two then told John, "That one's perfect for you and I'd love to watch." "I'm sure you're right," John said, double-checking, "but . . ." He shook his head back and forth.

DAVID

INSIDE OUT

I'm a talentless but popular young singer and I have the feeling
someone is watching me. I use the term loosely because I have
few feelings, and even they're too simple, like primary colors.
Fear is the basic one lately, no thanks to my nemesis (it could be
male, female, imaginary, ghost—I'm not big on subtleties)
poring over my every move, whether I watch TV, eat breakfast,
ride a bike, sleep, shower, go to school. . . . It's hard to describe
the sensation. Maybe rape or demonic possession come close. I
wouldn't know and I don't really care, to be perfectly honest.

The only thing that distracts me is fame, as in being onstage
or recording or having my photograph taken for one of those

21

teen magazines I'm the superstar of. I really am their star, meaning I'm on the covers, the foldout posters, and most of their articles focus on how great I look. I must be a great person, right? I think it follows. So why is this nemesis after me? What does it . . .? I can't . . . Oh, never mind. Sometimes I know how those Indians felt when they'd tie up some beautiful kid then invite God to take him or her like a Valium.

That's why I'm happy I'm famous for what I'm so famous for. Being gorgeous, I mean. It helps me believe in myself and not worry that I'm just a bunch of blue tubes inside a skin wrapper, which is what everyone actually is. I *am* gorgeous. That's not a brag. I can tell. People tell me so. I'm also friendly and sweet and naive except I do tend to talk way too much and I lie all the time. But you have to tell lies when somebody is judging you every minute. You have to cover yourself up with some kind of camouflage, even if that means bullshitting yourself. I do, in any case.

I turn my head and take a look at the boy to my left who has been staring at me this whole time. Of course he immediately glances away to make me think I'm mistaken, that he was daydreaming or I've been imagining everything. Maybe his eyes are the nemesis. That's the obvious solution except he's not looking at me anymore and I still feel all prickly and edgy and paranoid. Besides I think whoever's watching me's older. I can't believe guys in my age group hate other guys in this particular way. You know, like, "I want to force you to realize you're nothing special." It's too evil.

I can't tell if these students despise me or if they're so overly awed by the presence of someone this famous they can't decide what they could say that wouldn't sound idiotic. I hate their silence, in any case, and I wish school would be over. It almost is, actually, now that I look at the clock. I watch the time and nothing else until the exact point when school ends officially, then I stack up the textbooks I'd tossed on my desk a while back, fit them under my right arm and walk toward the spot where my dad's chauffeur always picks me up.

I'm walking straight ahead at the rectangle of sunlight that marks the end of the hallway. It looks like my bed because that's where I wish I was. Either that or a stage, where I'd also like to be, or a photographer's studio. Ditto. Sometimes when the afternoon sun hits my face I make believe a spotlight has been trained on me. For those glorious couple of seconds I don't care if someone can see through my image or even tries to. But I sure feel those evil eyes now, virtually setting my clothes on fire they want me dead or whatever so much. I'm running, even though people point and it never helps anyway.

I wish I could understand why I was picked for harassment. There are millions of people as cute as yours truly. I just got lucky in terms of my fame. It could have been that boy right there by the bus bench or someone in China. Maybe he feels it too, I mean the boy I just mentioned with dirty blond hair and a girlfriend. But he doesn't look spooked or antsy or anything. He looks as calm as a lake. Staring at him even lulls me a little. Mmm . . . Then all of a sudden his arm sticks out like the corpse's arm that stuck out of the lake in that movie *Deliverance*. He points at me and makes a snide remark I can't quite hear. And his girlfriend laughs.

Where's the chauffeur? Sometimes I think he arrives late on purpose to torture me. Or else my dad tells him to. My dad actually thinks if I get too much love I might never mature. Or something. He doesn't have any idea how cold these students can be and how sensitive I am to coldness. I think they call guys like me "hothouse flowers" because we can exist only in controlled situations. Stardom in my case. But it's hard here at

school because nobody cares. They think . . . I don't know what
they think. All I know is I can't stand the pressure another
minute.

It's different when I'm alone, in my bedroom let's say. Then I
just close my eyes and everything files very quietly into the
darkness inside my head, like my thoughts are a concert hall.
At the moment the world is too huge and unruly for me. Either
that or I'm terrified I'll see someone or something I don't want
to think about. So I'm shielding my eyes and counting seconds
off. You want to know what it's like? It's like when I was a kid I'd
wake up in the night feeling positive there was a murderer in my
room. But if I covered my head with a pillow and lay ultrastill,
I'd realize that he couldn't . . . Hey, great, there's the chauffeur
now!

Mmm . . . That's better. Let's see, where am I? How about a
photographer's studio? Blinding lights, backdrops, metallic
clicks, all that. I can't see the face of the man who's been hired
to perfect me, only a small piece of convex glass, in which I
come face-to-face with my distorted reflection. I look kind of
faint. Still, its contour soothes me like nothing else. I can block
that annoying thing out of my mind for a while. It's just one pair
of eyes among millions I'm trying to concentrate on. Maybe
they're more intense than most eyes. But they're drowned just
like everything else at the moment beneath the delight oozing
out of mine.

The photographer won't stop perfecting me. He says,
"Smile," I smile. He says, "Look sexy," I try. He just
announced that I look too emotional. I think, "How is that
possible?" I say, "I'm sorry." I close my eyes for a time, then
shake my head violently side to side. This succeeds in emptying

out my expression, but now my hair is a fright. A lady is called
from the sidelines and brushes my bangs back, then all the way
forward, then gradually into place. This interlude gives me a
chance to sing, so I will, in a rusty voice. Here goes nothing.

This is a song about how great I look. First, my hair, which is
brown, neatly cut and (I'll check) smells of herbal shampoo.
The aroma's outdoorish. I inherited puffy blue eyes from my
mother. I'll get them lifted someday. For now they seem sort of
lonely. My nose is petite but who cares as long as my lips, which
are truly enormous (they look like a tiny, skinned butt), don't get
too saggy. The face is oval shaped, naturally. My body's short,
thin, but healthy. It hangs from my shoulders like a clean leotard
and is just dead on its feet at the moment. The End.

Okay, I have time for one last, positively *last* number. It's
about sex, so you younger ones cover your ears, and it stars an A
& R man for a big record company. One day he's walking
downtown when he comes on a naive young boy who is thinking
out loud to himself. The man does a double take. The boy
thinks, "He's nice to have noticed me." They drive to the man's
place. After a couple of beers, he asks the boy to remove his
clothes. Then he pores over the body. He doesn't want to disturb
it, reinvent it or try to wear it himself. He wants to know where
that innocent voice could have come from. It came from a
perfect design. The End.

Right on cue I'm myself again. Or I look like what people
expect. The photographer puts down his camera, walks up to
me, takes a hand mirror out of his pocket and makes up two
lines of cocaine, which I snort, then smile into his lens again,
my eyes ecstatic and glittery, like they're reflecting a million
children's. A few more shots, another snort, then I sit at a table
directly across from the editor of a best-selling teen magazine
and sign some eight-by-ten photos of me that will appear in the

next issue. I write, "Let's run away, love, David," and "You're all I have, love you, David," and "Thinking of you, kisses, David," over and over. I don't mean any of this.

I'm only sincere when I forget who I am. Then I can stand or lie or whatever I wish, and sing, like my room is a huge microphone and I, the mouth of America's youth, am belting out its romanticized lyrics. But my life's become more and more mazelike, troublesome to define yet relentlessly sameish. I bounce between home, school, photographer, microphone, home, microphone, school, photographer, microphone, home and et cetera. I've learned a lot about one confined aspect of life, but, as with all minor artists, my subject (naiveté, as if one couldn't guess) is only interesting until I've said it all. Any minute now I'll say it all. Wait.

When I see myself in the future, which I try not to do, I think of someone like Fabian, my 1950s equivalent, who seems like heaven on earth in old film clips but, when you see him in person today, is a stooped, sagging child. He haunts the world, making folks like my mother, who claims she once swooned at the thought of him, whiten at how drab her youth looks, in retrospect. On the bright side, this means I'm a siren. I lure children into adulthood by mouthing inanities like, "I love you," when what I actually mean is, "You'll die someday." I'm totally evil. I want them to die. I want . . . I don't mean any of this.

I'm daydreaming. I find myself standing onstage in a beautiful pin spot. I've finished belting out one of my hits. From out of the shadowy sea of excitable kids climbs an older man. I think he's planning to rush up and hug me, but he draws a knife from his pocket. Before I can step back he's slashed at my face. Blood splatters onto his shirt. He carves, and uses his fingers to pull back the loose skin, until my whole skull is exposed to the air, and flesh hangs in waves around my neck like a Shakespearean collar. Then he steps back and squints like an artist appraising his work. I feel nothing, though I'm a little surprised when he shakes his head and sighs, "No, I wanted something else."

Enough of that. Now I'm posed on a set that's supposed to look human. Trash can to my left, graffitied wall to my right. I'm in the middle like Diana Ross, but I'm too insecure to sing. I'd only start making things up, such as I'm a night person. I sneak through dark alleyways, a slender shadow observing the rapes, robberies and lewd behavior of average Joes. I know what everyone really feels, and I respect that ambiguous inch between facial expression and soul. When I . . . Is that dad's voice yelling, "Dinner, Dave"? No. Where was I? Lies are so hard to keep track of. It's like you're constantly being reborn every time you begin a new sentence. Hey, I've got an idea.

Remember that song I sang a few minutes ago about how great I look? Here's the disco mix. My shoulders seem like a clothes hanger. I mean that as a compliment. They're very delicate. Think of the Golden Gate Bridge, which also tells you how handsome my tan is. My chest is bony. My stomach's so flat I sometimes joke I was born without entrails. My cock and balls are my own business. My ass has a permanent haze over it, like San Francisco or a dance floor. I can't see it. I only see images it suggests, say a Fabergé egg, the North Pole or a half-open door. My legs are reliable, to be unpicturesque for a moment. I'd draw an intimate portrait of my darling feet but my dad's yelling, "Dinner, Dave!" My feet look like dinner plates. How's that?

I'm back. I'm at dinner. My mom's sitting just to my left and my dad's on the other side of the table. He's a biologist. The house is full of these posters of nude boys and girls, all of whom have a chunk of flesh cut from their bodies (I hope they're just paintings). Dad not only loves to look into these wounds, he has memorized what's there. Somebody long ago named all those horrid blue tubes like they were pets. I guess that explains why I grew up averting my eyes from life's scary parts. For instance, over my dad's shoulder, I'm trying not to distinguish a boy about my age. His back is turned and where his ass used to be there's this thing that looks half like drawn curtains and half like what's left of a cow once it gets to the butcher's shop.

I've cut my quiche into eight thousand pieces. My dad could care less. He's too interested in the world. When he locates me in it he holds up the newspaper page and says, "Look, Dave." It's usually some piece using fame as a metaphor for how ridiculous things can become. I used to sulk, run upstairs, come back down, stab myself with a rubber knife. Now I cut the reviews out and Scotch-tape them into a scrapbook. I place compliments and cruel remarks on facing pages. Then I compare the impressions I leave. The critics who hate me are fairly articulate. The ones who adore me are shallow and indirect. What *is* a "dreamboat" exactly?

Why won't my champions say what they mean? All they do is describe me again and again in forgettable gushes. I wish I could talk to somebody about this. I know that's what parents are for. But the one time I felt strong enough to express myself fully . . . I came downstairs, tiptoed into the den (they were watching TV) and started saying how spooky it was to be worshiped by people with no taste, and how my voice was so tuneless and weak it took hours of studio trickery to make me listenable, and how my beauty was nothing but gift wrapping, that I was crazy and empty and . . .

"Know what I mean, Mom? Dad?" That's what I said at the time. Mom stuck her face in her gin glass. Dad just chirped, "Dave, rest assured your imagination is famous, at least in this household." Imagine my death for a second, them standing over my grave thinking, "We should've believed in him." That's what I think as I sit at the table tonight. If I was sure I'd be a legend in memory I'd run upstairs, lock my door and, well, I don't know what I might do, but it'd be serious. Trouble is, I'm dispensable. I try so hard to dig into myself, find blue anecdotes worth the world's time, but I just end up rattling on, using lie after lie to draw people's attention. . . .

Someone's ringing the doorbell. I know who it is. There's this boy at school, George, who I want to be friends with. He's terrific to look at, like me, and I have this idea if we sit and explore one another, both talkwise and physically, that'll quell you-know-what. It's still out there. I open the door, lead him into my room and flip the TV on, to warm the place up a bit. We watch cartoons for a half hour. Whenever I glance at him his face is so serious it's as if we've tuned in to a news program. Mine too, I imagine. Actually I watch him much more than I do the screen. It's amazing to be with someone who doesn't stare at me like I was taking my clothes off in front of a backdrop.

When we start to chat I detail myself. He seems impressed by the comings and goings. Of course I lie, since my schedule holds no tasty gossip. But even the wildest parts have an innate truth. You could say they were clarifications, like when you blow up a photograph until you see the ordered pattern of dots which compose it. Florid as I may become in description, I'm always simplistic deep down. Or I assume I am. That's what he's here to prove. But I've blabbed much too long and his eyelids are lowering over his eyes, as mine must be as well. "Listen," he yawns once I stop for a breath, "do you want to have sex or not?"

That's too blunt. Or is it? Would I ever say something so harsh? Well, I'm willing to try. "Yeah, let's fuck," I say. We have exactly the same high-pitched, colorless voices. And when we take off our clothes the parallels are unnerving. We become two little ghosts wearing human masks, nothing to look at below the neck, but sort of too cute from there up. Nevertheless, I reach my hand down and play with his highlights. I hate the fact that human bodies are warm. I think they should either be ice-cold or have no temperature whatsoever, like pieces of paper.

"Weird posters your dad's got downstairs." "What?" I say. "Oh, let's not think about them." But it's too late. I have my palm around his cock and balls and it strikes me that, whether he thinks so or not, it looks like someone cut a hole in his body and this is what gushed out. He's fondling mine with a real penetrating expression. If he had a pipe in his mouth, and his face filled out slightly then dropped an inch, he'd be my father in front of his "valuable" diagrams. He actually seems to be learning a thing or two, whereas I only see stuff his groin reminds me of: rotten fruit, a deflated balloon, ring of keys, stalactite . . . Enough of this.

I'm standing in front of a mirror, one hand on my genitals. I wish it were that simple. I mean, you know, like I'm being watched, as if the whole world is watching, like protesters said in the sixties, when I wasn't born yet. It wants me invisible. No, it wants my skin in a heap on the floor and a teetering skeleton smeared with blood. I can't imagine that. As far as I'm concerned, everything's out in the open. I won't become more realistic than this. I'm going to stand here awhile, bow my head, close my eyes, like we're told to in school when someone famous has died, and that's *it*. My mind's a total blank. Is a minute up yet?

Fine. Now it's my turn. I'm going somewhere where things transform into teentsy, unreachable stars (make that glitter) that look kind of sweet, but you don't have to think about what they imply. Bye, world. I stare at the walls. They start growing in every direction until my whole room is a mile wide and deep at least. I decorate it with thousands of blue plastic seats, and them with expectant young faces. My bed's growing too. It resembles a stage. Set discreetly on top, I envision a figurine bathed in a spotlight. It's holding a microphone in its right hand. It starts to open its mouth. I can't wait to completely refill myself with its opaqueness.

"Hi, it's nice to be back. You look perfect. So, how do *I* look?" Ten thousand boys and girls, mostly the latter, respond. They seize any chance to reflect what I've given them. I give them love in a form they can understand, but all they seem to be able to do in return is howl like some immense dog. In thanks, I shake a few hands that jut out of the darkness. My touch ripples back through the concert hall until the whole room is howling again. That's enough love for now. "I think you know this first song." Sure they do. Howl, they say, as I position myself center stage, formalizing our balanced relationship.

Behind my back there are five men. Each is in charge of a musical instrument. I think of them as machinery. I turn them on with a prearranged signal. My glance usually does the trick. They were chosen to structure my background because they're proficient and ugly, qualities which reinforce my distinctiveness. They represent the world, slightly romanticized. My job involves a belief in our metaphor, something I've never achieved, but the fact that I've dreamt up an interesting script seems to satisfy all concerned. Here comes the part where I have to act human. "You were alone when we met / and your smile told me something / I'll never forget / With your hand held in mine / I will never forget / our very first time . . ."

Now I remember why I took this role in the first place. It's a great place to hide, much like being invisible. Kids don't have any idea what's in front of them. If I could read their minds it would go something like this: "He's so cute and romantic and lonely. He makes me think love is a virtuous thing. One day I'll bump into him and explain that I know how he feels. He'll be amazed by my clarity. Suddenly all the anonymous "yous" in his songs will be filled with my name. He'll cry. We'll run off together. The sun will shine, blah, blah, blah." Meanwhile I'm thinking how silly they are not to look in the obvious place.

Here. I'm right here, inside this. ". . . Our love is forever / I'm there when you call / Just believe in our first time / That's all, that's all." I finish my part of the number. The band plays the melody all by themselves. I bow my head, the idea being I'm too emotional. Cue the howl. Now I raise my chin, let them know all's not lost. I expect to see blinding lights, but what I actually find is a girl running at me, full speed. I step aside just in time and she flies by my right shoulder, crashing into the bass player. He and the girl look embarrassed. He throws her away. She hurls around, trying to spot me. A bodyguard drags her astonished face into the darkness. Howl!

"Thanks very much. Do you like to dance? I do." I prove my point, begin bouncing all over the stage in a vaguely symmetrical pattern. The band tries to re-create one of the cuts on my latest LP. Its lyrics are hard to invest with sincerity. "Don't sit at home / Go out / Show the world / what you're all about . . ." The real me would never relax like this. Pretending that love's just a matter of asking for help is a big enough lie in itself, but trying to make kids believe they can wipe away all of their troubles by shaking their hips? Well, it's just an excuse to display my ass. I'm wearing skintight white pants. The assembled scream shrilly, like they've seen a ghost, but they're probably thinking of snowfall or cats.

When I was a little boy there was this band called The Doors. Their lead singer, like me, was aware that his fans were in love with whatever he did. But, unlike me, his fans were horny adults. When they looked at his body they actually wanted to fuck it. One time at a concert he thought, "Let's give them what they want." He pulled down his pants, or so the story goes. There was the truth: cock, balls, ass. But instead of gang-raping him, his fans got bored and stopped buying his records. He put on weight, went to Paris and kicked off. I could repeat his mistake, but I won't. Well, let's just say it's a fleeting temptation. The song's over.

"Sometimes I feel so alone, but just knowing you're there makes me happy. This song's dedicated to you." Each of the stage lights, excluding a pin spot aimed right at my face, fades to black. My head's a moon shining down on their dreamy thoughts. "When I'm low / when I can't think of which way to go / you're somewhere out in the crowd / Yes, I know . . ." I didn't write these ingenuous words. They were sold to me for an unquotable price, then I rehearsed them until they appeared to describe my emotions. But if their emotions were mine I wouldn't be where I am. I'd be out in the audience, familiarizing myself with the way I feel, instead of processing somebody else's clichés. I guess it's a testament to my intelligence that I can edit myself out of life, though it leaves me a little upset by the sight of my own shadow. Who does it really belong to, this mannequin I'm so adept at portraying or . . .?

Time for another hit. This one's a toughy. I've been able to squeak my way through so far, but this melody's too difficult for my voice. Backstage three men are hunched over a top-secret microphone, singing along with me. When the tune arcs too high or dips too low I move my lips and they fill in the hole with a passionate wail I'm incapable of. My fans, excited by this seeming burst of emotion, jump out of their seats and pack themselves up against the stage. I slink about, an inch or two from their grasp. ". . . There's a place in my heart / that nobody can see / and it tears me apart / when you look at me . . ." Suddenly a chubby girl leaps onstage and heads for me. When she's a few feet away she realizes I'm lip-synching, skids to a stop and claps her hand to her mouth. Just then a bodyguard grabs her around the waist. Howl!

That was close. Five songs to go, with some patter between. The first four go smoothly. I mouth their shallow ideas with the help of my mystery voices, and punctuate the procession with handshakes, brief flashes of my famous backside, some spins, eight blown kisses. When I get to the ballad I pick out a girl who looks especially moved and allow her to guess she's the "you" of my lyric. I'm always embarrassed to use this trick. It seems the slightest bit evil. All the loneliness she's ever felt explodes out of her eyes. "Don't let it end here," she undoubtedly thinks. "You're the one / I've been waiting to meet / Love was a dream / Now it's so sweet . . ." For the rest of the concert she grins at me knowingly, as if she's in on the hoax. How pathetic.

"I'll never forget tonight. You've been my favorite audience. It's hard to say goodbye, but . . ." They howl. I start the last number, my biggest hit to date. "Saying goodbye / without asking why / Yet I'll always remember you / until the day I die . . ." That encapsulates it, and, though I'm so tired I practically creak through my dance steps, I know they no longer care how good I am. They're blending in with my wallpaper pattern. But, as they dissipate, there's an attempt to embrace me. It's some older man, clambering onto what's left of the stage. Where's my bodyguard? The man draws a knife from his pocket and floats over. Luckily, before he gets very far, he turns into my table lamp. I reach out and turn it off.

*   *   *

I'm completely exhausted. The world is pitch-dark and ambig-uous, unlike my audience. I cross its mind and it stops what it's doing for two or three minutes, in awe of what it would undress were it granted one wish. I lie inside what it thinks of me, an expensively wrapped gift, wishing somebody would open me up and let us know if I'm really a famous young singer or little more than a gag. Or am I just a bomb, a shiny thing crammed with blood, guts and bones, whose tiny word balloon reads, "Don't get close"? I'm going to cry if I keep this up.

Any minute now there'll be a knock at my door. My dad will stumble in, bump his way through the furniture, kiss my fore-head, thinking I'm fast asleep, and say good night, in a gin-soaked voice. Because my eyes will be closed I'll imagine it's anyone, everyone, wishing me well. It'll distract me from my repetitive thoughts for a second. He'll sort of open his mouth and whisper something so gentle and thoughtless I'll actually fall asleep, lulled by the sound. That amazes me. Right now I can say it's a trick, but when he's here I'll be inert.

Until then, here's what I want. Love. Specifically, I want the power to make people love me. Maybe a secret word which I'd only use when I saw someone special. I'd walk up to him or her, say that word, and he or she would be very in love with me. Then, if they ever got bored, there'd be another word that would cancel the spell, wipe their memories clear of me. I could be anywhere and when I saw someone special I'd walk up to him or her, say the word, and he or she would forget what they'd planned to do. If I said, "Come home with me," they'd follow. We'd be together right now, in this very bed.

What could I offer them? Here's a list. Nervous, wealthy, at home, half-asleep, cute, confused . . . That's as far as I get. Oh, contrived and talkative. I guess those words also go in there. Now I'm supposed to take that puny list, stretch it out like a tightwire and walk very slowly across. Or something. I'll probably dream that I'm doing so, if I can fall asleep. Then I'll wake up and see this bedroom again. The End. I like how in movies that phrase will just suddenly appear at a certain point. Most children worship a statue of some guy nailed up on a cross. I worship The End. It's a great concept.

I'm talking in circles. That's not a clever ploy, really. Maybe somewhere in the back of my mind I hope speaking like this might hypnotize the world so I can slip away. But, first of all, I'm just limited. No matter how I extend myself I don't get closer to who I am, which, I admit, is my ultimate goal. I could look into a mirror all night, or lie here, eyes shut, projecting my body all over the place, and I'd still wind up making things up until death has been slammed in my face. That's pretentious.

I've been pretending my whole life. As a baby I'd do anything for a pat on the head. As a boy I would act out my father's appraisals ("cute," "darling," "doll-face," "exquisite") as if they were simple commands, since those words were the only things I had to play with. In my early teens, boys and girls flocked around. When I asked them why, they gave out long strings of adjectives. Ditto now, except my new "friend," that nemesis, is so vague I can't understand what it says when it tries to dissect me. All I feel, like I said, is this fear which I'm learning to live with.

What other choice have I got? That guy George, my parallel self or whatever? Next time I see him at school, I'll go over and try to be boyfriends. I realize I'm deluded. Sure, he's a new place to check my appearance in. Maybe our slight resemblance has something to say for itself. But I'm sure if I get too close, do the explorer bit, I'll find the same old stuff. Blood, guts, bones, not much else. I could pick through that mess for the rest of my days without any results, despite what my dad thinks. He also thinks beauty is "useless fluff." He scribbled that in the steam on my mirror once. Honest.

I just heard the door open. Someone is walking unsteadily through the dark. Must be my father. In some ways I wish it was anyone else, but I'm so wired it seems like the only way I'll ever sleep is if he does what I've come to love. There's that word again. I shouldn't use words I don't understand. I should just let it happen. Footsteps, the banging around as he hits certain pieces of furniture, and now the smell of gin close to my face. He kisses me. His voice sounds halfhearted when he says good night, but there's no one else here so it must be the truth, insincere or not. Does that make any sense? I'm going under.

Before I do, here's a very last song, though I'm too tired to give it much gusto. It's about me and I wrote it myself. I know that's like saying a mannequin's smile has a basis in thought, but here goes. Once upon a time I was a little boy. I rode my bike constantly. I wandered everywhere, bought stuff, sang songs to myself. I stopped in a mall. This man came up to me. He was an A & R man for a big record company. He told me I was amazing. I said okay and we went back to his house. He tried to fuck me. I bled all over the place. Then he showed me the door and said, "Thanks for being so well designed, kid."

That was supposed to be funny, but I was in pain for a month. I'm sure he doesn't remember the incident. Still, I can't forget. Maybe his gaze is what's sifting through me at the moment. I know that's too anticlimactic. Anyway, it's a pretty good song, right? It seems to have sprung from a life that was long and productive, and, with the same breath, it's quick paced like mine. That's my guess. All it needs is a really spectacular ending, but I'm too exhausted to figure one out. The best I can do is the relative truth. I lie here on my bed, tossing this way and that in the stupid belief sleep will straighten me out. But first I'll set the alarm.

GEORGE

THURSDAY, FRIDAY, SATURDAY

George looked at a poster for Saturday's dance. It was too badly drawn. Were those people's faces or not? He had to tilt his head to get the information. "At least it's colorful," he mumbled, wishing he had a few felt-tips himself. He'd make one twice as weird. "Wonder who drew it?"

Footsteps. It was Mr. Reed. "I said go straight to the office," he yelled, grabbing George's arm. "Now!" George let himself be dragged off, arms and legs flailing about. He thought of how vulnerable he would appear from a distance. But the halls were deserted.

"Yes?" sighed a man George assumed was the principal. Mr.

Reed pointed at George. "He has been sleeping in class all semester. I can't do a thing with him." George shut his eyes so he wouldn't look bored. That way he'd feel what these assholes believed he should.

George imagined a clockface. It read three-thirty P.M. A bell rang. A school bus pulled up to his feet. Its doors swung open. "So, Miles," the principal said, "do you have a suggestion?" George thought a second. "Transfer me into McGough's class." He opened his eyes a crack. Reed looked hurt.

Tick-tick-tick-tick-tick. "You can go." Taking a couple of books from his locker, he stood on the sidewalk in front of the school. Ten minutes passed. A blue van pulled up. "Where to?" The driver had long straight black hair and a moustache. There was an old mattress slung in the back with a collie on top.

"Like school?" the driver asked. "When it doesn't get in my way," George said. "I hated it, but it makes sense in retro-spect." "Well," George said, "I'll let you know." The driver laughed. He seemed okay, if a little too into the hippie shit. The peace symbol paperweight around his neck was a joke.

They talked. George let out some info. Rich parents, Disney-land, grass, acid, only child, gay. They shared a joint. ". . . I like my dad," George went on, "but I don't have much choice. See, my mother's so sick all the time. That's the turn just ahead."

The van pulled next to the curb. The driver put it in park. "Why don't we . . . ?" He gestured out at the road. George thought his eyes were a shade too erotic. "Uh, no . . . home-work." George clutched his books. "Call me," the guy said, handing George a card. It read, "Chuck Roosevelt, Carpentry." "Maybe." George meant that.

George knocked three times on his mom's bedroom door, thinking she wouldn't hear. "G-George?" He went in and eased himself down on the bed. They never spoke much. His words were hard on her. She'd "love to talk" but the struggle might polish her off. He watched her face twist and turn like a special effect.

When he felt awkward just sitting there, he kissed her shiny gray forehead. Kissing her left him weak. Back in his room, he had to waste a whole joint getting over it. Part of him knew she should die and leave others alone. But he wanted to kill himself when he realized that. Things were incredibly fucked up.

"Dead . . . men . . . tell . . . no . . . tales." George said those words with a fake British accent. He'd heard them spoken that way in his favorite Disneyland ride. Repeating the line six or seven times cheered him up. He told himself he'd experienced death.

It half worked. He sat up in bed and thought of calling the carpenter's house. At least he'd be out and about. Sex was distracting, even if who he'd be having it with was a bore. "Hi, Chuck . . ." ". . . Great, George. I'll pick you up around six. Bring a warm coat."

"I'm having dinner out," George told his dad when he heard the familiar knock. Mr. Miles parted the door a crack. George confirmed he'd done his homework. School was fine. He'd opened the window because it felt good, not to cover up anything. "Yeah, I'll be back by eleven." "I love you, George." "Likewise, Dad."

Chuck drove them into the hills. George knew the spot. "Cocaine Flats," as somebody had dubbed it. At the end of the steep, winding road was a parking lot. Great view of twinkling lights. Total privacy. Cops could be seen miles off, grass ditched or pants zipped up. No sweat.

Chuck led George down a trail littered with beer cans. No one was on the big slab of cement. It stank of piss. Chuck lit a joint.

"You're an incredibly beautiful boy," he said. George cracked up. Smoke tooted out of his nose. Chuck leaned over and kissed the tight, hazy grin.

George felt a hand swim around in the front of his underpants. He liked the feeling of being plugged up. Sloppy tongue down his throat, fingernail in his piss-slit, two fingers up his ass. Chuck shook a little and came on his stomach. "Lick it off." George did.

Chuck drove. George stared straight ahead. "Please," Chuck whispered, "don't tell your folks or . . ." George shook his head. ". . . I didn't mean to freak you out." George nodded. He didn't know what he felt, but there were tears in him somewhere. "Let me out," he managed. "I'll walk."

George turned to a page in his diary and wrote: "Today I felt sick or tense or something else. Pressure in head and chest. Aren't I ever going to get back to normal, or what I remember of that? But no one else seems to give a fuck, so I shouldn't.

"My friends bore me. I ate lunch with Sally and she pissed me off. Paul was fine for a while but I got too fed up. That David person keeps trying to get me in bed. I'm considering that. My decent mood has changed into a weird feeling. Intense.

"I got thrown out of class today. I'll try harder tomorrow. Right. Smoked grass this evening and it ruined my thinking. I realize how screwed up and closed off my feelings and personality are in my dealings with people. Don't have a solution though.

"I allowed this guy Chuck to have sex with me. I did it because it was something to do, not because I admired him. I was like something he wanted to buy but couldn't really afford. I know that's stupid. He doesn't even know me or want to.

"I was afraid to let go, or I felt like this pretty thing with a few rips in it. I wanted him to get rid of me. He did, but he apologized too much. He wasn't strong and that upset me. I'm not sure why, except the obvious.

"I'd like to get away, meet some new people, stop smoking grass all the time, get closer to my feelings. I cut them off for a while. That felt better at first, then worse. I'm confused but not worried for some reason. It'll work out, I tell myself."

Rrrrring. "George Miles, please stay after class a few minutes." The room emptied out. Mr. McGough asked why George had been transferred. "I think I'm just too imaginative." "I admire that in a youngster," the teacher smiled, "but put your *skills*—shall we say—where they'll benefit both of us. That's all I ask."

He patted George's head. "Okay, take off." George paused in the doorway, bit his lip. "You like movies?" he asked. "Some of them, naturally." "Maybe we could go see one this weekend or something." "Why, you lonely?" Mr. McGough made a pouty face. "That's not what I meant," George said. "Fuck it. Never mind."

George saw his former girlfriend at a lunch table. "Hey, McGough's great," she said, mouth full of meat loaf. "Yeah," George yawned, "he seems okay if a little too into himself." "He's a real poet, George. You can't expect guys like that to be generous." She fished around in her notebook. "Read this."

It was a poem of Mr. McGough's. Titled "Paler, Smaller, Less Touching," it seemed to be about love but was much, much too wordy. All George could see was a bunch of stuff mixed inexplicably. "It's fine." He handed it back to her. "Let's smoke a joint."

They crawled under the green football bleachers. She kissed his sweaty cheek. He knew she still liked him, even if they hadn't fucked in months. He'd made his own feelings perfectly clear just the weekend before. "I know," she'd sighed. "You like boys, at least for *now*, right?"

They passed the joint back and forth, looking out at the football field. George thought its dry, trampled acres looked beautiful. He had a fondness for empty things normally filled up with people. Abandoned houses, parking lot structures on Sunday nights, holograms, telephone booths . . .

"You'll be at the dance, I hope?" George nodded, lighting another joint. "Mr. McGough will be one of the chaperones," she told him. Pleased as he was by this news—it would give them a chance to talk and maybe something else—he made his face look unbearably bored, a favorite pastime of late.

"I'm going to make a prediction," she said in a trembling voice. "You and Mr. McGough will be boyfriends by Sunday." "You're just jealous," he said. "No, I think you'd be handsome together." George thought it out. The guy was clever, artistic, sarcastic and . . . "I don't know, Sally. I'm too stoned to argue about it."

George daydreamt his way through the rest of his classes. In Art I he put a few drops of black paint on a large sheet of paper and smeared them around with his thumb. That was the day's high point, although it got him an F. He was walking to bus #12 when he heard a familiar voice. "George, wait a sec."

Mr. McGough said he'd give him a ride. It was a black Ford with bucket seats, large enough for a family. "You married?" "Used to be, but I don't think a commitment's the right thing for me." "Hey, I heard you partake," George said, pulling a joint from his pencil case. Mr. McGough pushed the lighter in.

While they smoked, Mr. McGough talked a lot about New

York ("heavenly"), rock bands he liked ("ones with rough edges"), grass he had smoked in New Guinea once ("brilliant"), how TV rots people's minds to the beauty of language. George watched his face. It was a sunbaked wreck but sort of young underneath.

"Thanks," George said, slamming the door. "See you Saturday night." "No doubt," Mr. McGough grinned. He gunned it. As the car sped out of sight George put a hand to his forehead. He was about to do something inane like cry. "Now what?" He lowered onto the driveway.

A hand touched his shoulder. "Are you okay down there?" George burst into tears. He struggled up and threw himself at the man's chest. "I love you. Shit," he sobbed. But when he saw the tattoo of a battleship he tried to free himself. "No problem, honey," his dad whispered. "Let it loose."

"Why am I such a waste? I don't care about anything. I used to, really, a lot. I could make people like me and they'd come back here and I'd show them the stuff in my room. It was great.

"I was thinking of John today. I really liked him, but he only likes art. That David asshole keeps bugging me. I've decided he's nuts. Sally told me he's not a rock singer at all, just a liar. I think she's in love with him.

"I don't know what's going on. I keep crying for no reason. Now I'm hung up on this teacher. He seems nice, but I'm not sure he is. I know it's because he's a friend of John's. Not that I want to see John again. It's just, oh, fuck it.

"I wish I knew what I wanted. I'm still trying all sorts of stuff and when the right thing shows up I'll keep doing it. Sometimes I think drugs are better than anything else, but I'd still like to stop them. Sure. Forget it.

"I saw this movie on TV tonight that made me think a lot. It was about this boy's death. He was like me. He took drugs and all that. The way he acted when he smoked a joint was a joke, but it wasn't too bad when he started to think death was great.

"The best part was when he took acid and thought he was dead. He saw these neat-looking skeletons who said, 'We're you,' and pointed down at their bodies. It scared him, but I would have stayed with them. It looked more fun than his life.

"Now it's late. I hear Mom's chest all the way through the wall. It sounds like the ocean. I guess I should go to sleep. There's no school tomorrow, thank God. Maybe Mr. McGough will fall in love with me. Sure. That's stupid. I know that."

The gym looked spectacular. Colored lights pinpointed certain spots—dance floor, refreshment stand, makeshift stage—but left the rest unimportant. George looked at it for a while, then he put the orange acid chip under his tongue. "Goodbye, cruel world," he thought.

Sweaty hands covered his eyes. "Sally?" They were withdrawn. "Nice guess," Paul smiled. Then they yelled in each other's ears. "Music sounds great this loud," Paul bellowed. "I feel like I'm inside a tiger's mouth." George would have used the word "battleship." He felt like dancing. "Seen Sally?"

"No way." Paul shook his head. "Got any drugs?" he added. George shook his head. "Just what I'm already on." "Well, I'm on a drug run, so see you, man." "Later," George said. He scanned the room. He couldn't see faces, just smeared ovals. "She'll find me," he thought.

There was Mr. McGough. George recognized his suit. George rose and made his way through, sometimes accidentally bumping into, some people he vaguely knew. If they were greeting him he couldn't tell. Still, he was pretty sure Mr. McGough licked his lips when their eyes met.

"Hey, George," the teacher said. He led them into a quieter part of the gym. "I trust you, don't I?" George nodded. "I've gotten access to the coach's lounge." He pointed a finger at George. At its end, swinging back and forth like a pendulum, was a big ring of keys. "You and I . . . ?"

George licked his lips. "I get the picture," he smirked. Inside the office, Mr. McGough felt around on a cluttered desk, found a lamp. It lit up Coach Burke's diploma and an old snapshot of him in red swim trunks. "Once that fat blob was a knockout," George thought. "Yuck."

"Prepare yourself for a charming surprise," said a sexy voice. George settled back on the desk top. He felt his ass squish against it. He gripped the trimming. His knuckles turned purple. He shut his eyes. He parted his lips wide enough that a tongue could fit through them.

George thought, "If God made a visit to earth it'd be in the form of a kiss. Being kissed by someone I admire is the closest I've gotten to peace on earth, like Xmas carolers sing. God would give each boy a taste of His lips then go back to whatever dimension He hides in. That would help."

What a whacked-out idea. George liked how acid could blow up the flimsiest topic. Just then a sharp object scraped through his lips. His eyes flipped open. Mr. McGough put a match to its other end. "Pure Nicaraguan," he said. "Go ahead. Blow your brains out."

Two minutes later they edged through the door. The dance floor was a blur. Its details had blended together, a greenish white. It made George think of a Xmas tree, flocked, lying down on its side. He was afraid he'd get cut if he entered it. "Come meet some people, kid." "Huh? Oh, right."

"This is Maureen Kendrick, a wonderful talent. And these are some friends of hers. Uh . . ." "Alex," one muttered. "Cliff," said the other. Their faces were featureless, like outer space helmets. "Now we'll be off," announced Mr. McGough. He pinned George in a headlock. Cliff yelled goodbye like he meant it.

The dance petered out. George spent the last hour sitting alone by an unlighted tennis court. He felt too high to make sense, especially to himself. Mr. McGough had gone somewhere with John. "Hell, I hope," George said wistfully. "I hate their guts." He stared up at the moon, tried to read its lips.

"You would accept a ride home?" said a voice with a heavy French accent. "I can't talk," George whispered. But, slightly curious, he turned his head. It was a stranger of some sort. "Philippe," the guy said, stuck one hand out. His ring had an ivory skull on it.

He guided George to a Porsche. George reclined in the back and faked sleep. When the car stopped he roused himself. It was his house, but the lights were on. He didn't want to be seen at the moment. He checked Philippe's eyes. They were nuts. Perfect. "Take me away from this."

Dark leaked through the blinds. George took a sip of his screwdriver. Philippe didn't talk much, nor make any sense when he did. George was too loaded to do more than comment on stuff. He'd already said he liked everything in the house. He thought, "I'm passing out."

"You are mine tonight." George slowly opened his eyes. "Would you like to know how?" George shrugged. "Just do it," he yawned. "No, I need you to know. I watched you bend over an hour ago and your Levi's were tight to your ass. I saw the crack. It is so wide and deep."

George almost laughed. He took a drink instead. "Think how the glass is your crack." George giggled. "Think that you are in the desert. This alcohol is the last you will have for a year." George stuck out his tongue. "Good. Put it into the drink." "Great sense of humor," George thought.

"You notice those ice in the drink? That is your shit. Take one into your mouth." "Jesus," George muttered, sliding the smallest cube through his lips. "Hold it there. I want your mouth very cold." George glanced up. Sure enough, the guy had actually said that.

"Yes, good, now lie on the rug." George set his glass down and sprawled on his back. "Relax. Open your mouth. Loose your fists." George heard the floor creak. A shadow fell over his face. One of Philippe's hands encircled his wrist, raised that arm, let it drop.

Hands started roaming all over his clothes. First they followed the shape of his skeleton, inching along, like it was covered with braille or something. Now they took hold of his crotch, separated his cock from his balls, then the balls from each other. *"Drôle de ménage!"* Philippe said.

"That's a compliment," George guessed. Just then a cock clogged his throat. Skin and pubic hair smothered his face. It made him think of the pirate mask he used to wear every Halloween. He concentrated on that fun idea, and did his best not to think of Philippe, who was patting him down like a cop.

The cop yanked his pants off. A hand scooped his balls up. A fingertip poked them around in their sack. They rolled badly, like footballs. George wondered how that looked. He'd never paid much attention to how he was built, thinking that was for others to like or dislike.

The acid chip hadn't worn off after all. George tried to imagine the things on his body. He saw a sparse-looking skinny kid. He played with its crotch like he was a cat and it a rubber mouse. When that got boring he rolled the kid over. Flop.

The fantasy's sharp lines began to blur. He knew he was stroking his own ass, but he couldn't define its appearance. What he did see was too nonspecific. He opened it. "Why did I do that?" he wondered. His thoughts had a very slight echo. He faded out. "Where was I?"

He was an old miner pointing his gas lantern into a cob-webbed shaft. He scratched one dirt-caked, stubbly cheek and pushed his hat back. Far down the passageway, covered with dust, a small skeleton swung, tinkling in a rotted noose. He took his lamp in and cut it loose.

George blinked, attempting to stop the hallucination. He'd accidentally shit. He tried to rise up. "No," Philippe shouted, "that is what I wanted to happen!" His voice sounded pre-recorded. George tried to do what he always did when life grew too realistic. He made up a Disneyland ride and rode through it.

This one was honestly scary. It wended its way through a dark, barren tunnel that kept getting smaller and smaller. Occasionally skeletons fell from the roof and cracked in slivers around him. A heavily accented voice was saying really weird things, like, "You are dead, baby." "Ouch!" The ride ended.

George didn't mind being fucked. That was business as usual. But the aroma of shit was disgusting. As soon as Philippe got his rocks off, George ran to the bathroom and puked for at least a half hour. "I never want to have sex again," he moaned. "Period."

He took a shower. He thought about things. They added up. He started crying. It wasn't easy to stop, but he managed. He made a face at himself in the mirror. "Jerk." When he got back to the living room, Philippe was waving around an air freshener. That made him cry again.

He struggled into his clothes, stopping every few seconds to wipe his nose, dry his eyes. When he got to the door, Philippe strolled up. "You are very beautiful," he said. George shook his head. "You fascinate me." George shrugged. He opened the door. It was dawn. The light hurt his eyes a bit.

CLIFF

THE OUTSIDERS

George looked like he was sleepwalking. Something was wrong. He said he wouldn't know how to describe it. At first taking acid three times a week helped. Then he'd relied on our little talks. Now there was nothing between him and "it," as he called what he currently felt. "It's getting worse," he remarked as we strolled hand in hand through a city park.

I understood what he meant. "It" was as vague as that sentence. In other words, I'd never grasp it. Saying so wouldn't help. Friends were just light entertainment at best. I kept my ears open, exaggerated my interest, and hoped compassion would strike him as sexy at some point. "Let's sit," he sighed when our eyes met.

His hand was cold. Otherwise I might have thought I was walking around with my shadow. One time I turned and examined his eyes on the off chance he'd started OD'ing. I wanted to read his mind, but all I saw was some dry leaves get larger and larger, then shatter like miniature fireworks beneath his shoes.

"I'm feeling totally weary, for one thing," he said. We'd situated ourselves on a grassy slope. The day had cooled. A light breeze came up from the parking lot. His eyes were so shadowed they looked like dark glasses. His lips were so full and red they seemed magnified. His chin was balancing atop one knee, his arms wrapped loosely around that particular leg.

"George, stay at my place tonight." I knew that sounded too matter-of-fact. I wanted to fuck him. That was my goal, but I couldn't decide how to phrase it. "I can't, I'm seeing Philippe." "Foreigners first," I huffed, and accidentally kicked a small hole in the grass. George was scanning the clouds. "*You* explain it," he shrugged, knowing I couldn't.

I couldn't even imagine us fucking without a lump in my throat. So every night when I lowered my eyelids, I pictured George and Philippe instead. It looked like a scene from *The Blob*. George tripped and, as he fell, a flabby body just swallowed him up. I'd arch my back and come, dazed by the strange combination of lust and petty loss I felt.

Now George was sitting right next to me, staring up at a cloud bank. I couldn't guess how to get him in bed, much less save him from "it." At least in fantasies I'd had some kind of effect on him, though he would never know how, when, where, what. "I should go home. I'm just boring you." "No, you're not," I whispered. "Well," he said, "I'm boring myself."

"I'll see you later," he yelled as he trudged up his front walk. I threw my car into drive and gunned it, searching for him in my rearview mirror. He'd stopped dead in his tracks and was watching me barrel off, arms wrapped around his chest, sure he had pissed me off. "Shit," I said, gripping the wheel, "no matter what I do . . ."

I climbed the stairs to my room. Mom had cleaned the house. The air smelled poisonous. I set an old Bryan Wisdom LP on the turntable. There was a song on its second side called "Note to No One," in which the deeply depressed singer/songwriter moaned out some personal problems to a dead friend. It was a joke, in particular one couplet.

When it approached I sat forward. ". . . I'm as made up as the TV star my lover's ogling / I feel like an empty exercise in acting . . ." That was so ludicrous. Why did it make me want to cry? Maybe because he'd grown so out of touch with his thoughts, he was forced to use strained images to suggest the extent. I could relate to that kind of approach. Still, every now and then, it helped to brush up.

The phone rang. "It's George. You're down on me, aren't you?" I said I wasn't. He sounded like he'd been crying. He claimed he hadn't, although he admitted he'd tried. "I want to help you, George." "Well," he said, and took a breath that sounded more like a hiccup, "you may." I let him sob for a while. The only words he could manage were, "Maybe . . . it's . . . all this . . . Philippe . . . stuff."

I tried to find the right tone. "Why not just say it," I thought. But before I could blurt that cliché I'd longed to air all these months, I decided his tears were a great opportunity. "I understand you, George. Give me less than a minute to think." I felt a weird grin spread over my face as I said this.

Once he'd calmed down I suggested a plan. I'd follow him to Philippe's. I'd hide outside and observe their sex. Afterward we'd go somewhere and I'd give him my honest opinion on what it meant. "Yeah, I guess so," he sighed, "but you'll be shocked." "No," I said. I grabbed a loose sheet of paper and scribbled down the directions. "Okay, got it."

I crawled through some bushes, careful to keep them from rustling. I found an unshuttered window and rose to my feet. The room was plush, overfurnished in shades of white. Philippe sat on a black sofa. He was ashen faced, a little gray at the temples and saggy. To his left George was stumbling out of his Jockey shorts. Above their heads hung a charcoal drawing of somewhere that didn't exist.

I scooped some dirt off the sill and got my balance. Cars driving by couldn't see me. The lawn was deep, the foliage thick. The room was subtly lit, like a case full of perishable objects. I wished I'd brought my old Konica. I could have gotten some great shots of George in the nude. As I'd hoped, he was so pale and smooth he looked airbrushed.

He shut his eyes and felt his way through the furniture, stubbing a toe now and then. He ended up by a small air conditioner, turned in slow circles for thirty seconds or so, then lay facedown on the rug's smoky pattern. Philippe rose from his chair and knelt over the body. I thought, "Religious," but what happened next made me think of a porn film I'd fidgeted through.

In the film a blond lay on her stomach. A fat man pried open her ass, stuck out his tongue and spread her privates with spit from the pale pubic bush to the small of her back, repainting the same exact spots until they caught the light, appeared monstrous one second, toylike the next.

Philippe's tongue had a similar sweep. It climbed the rubble of George's balls, swabbed the crack and returned to base over and over. At first that looked too mechanical, then I was struck by the figures' grace. In comparison my fantasies were a scrawl. I nearly blushed at the thought of subjecting this boy to them.

George got a spanking. Philippe's arm seemed to move in slow motion, but I heard the slaps, even through plate glass. After a dozen he eased off, smiled down at his handprints and mouthed a few words. The asshole swelled, trembled, then very slowly produced a turd. It rose an inch in the air, toppled into his waiting palm.

I thought I could make it, but halfway down the street I splayed my hands on the nearest tree and threw up. A dog walked over, sniffed my splattered Adidas. "Go fuck yourself," I moaned. It backed off a few feet and watched me retch for a while with its confused eyes. Wondering how the dog felt helped get my mind off my misery.

I thought of the first and last time I'd gone riding. Horses resembled big dogs to me, with even kinder smiles. Dad helped me onto one's back. It tore off down the trail. I gripped the reins tighter the more it squealed and tried to buck me off. Suddenly I lurched face-first toward the earth. The bored dog barked, trotted under a hedge.

Somehow I got to my car. Its chilly metal felt perfect. I lay on the hood taking deep, even breaths. After a while I stood up. I was still much too shaky to form an opinion of what I'd seen. On the one hand, I longed to find some sort of clinic and have my memory flushed. On the other, I wanted to ring Philippe's bell, shake his hand and say, "Yeah, right."

I drove into a Shell station and phoned my friend Alex. He was the most callous, sarcastic person I knew, but we'd been friends since tenth grade. He knew me inside out. "We have to talk." I gave a quick sketch of what I'd seen. "Rush over here," he gasped. Ten minutes later I eased past two sleepy-eyed parents and into his bedroom. "So, tell all." I pulled a chair up.

I loved seeing Alex. His face was covered with freckles, ten deep in some places. They camouflaged his quite commonplace features with startling images. I could connect up the dots and see galloping horses, a black man lifting a crate, a map of Oregon . . . It was the ideal appearance for someone so witty and complex.

Tonight I was too self-absorbed to see anything. I talked. He nodded occasionally. "Phew!" he said once I'd completed my tale. "Little George Miles? I can't reconcile that." He crossed his arms and seemed lost in thought. I must have drifted off because the next thing I saw was a mouth smeared with tooth-paste. "Rise and shine, pervert," it said.

While Alex showered I reached behind his cassette deck. I found the baggie where he hid his grass, rolled a joint, struck a match on my belt buckle. I tried the radio. Out popped Sparks' "Amateur Hour," a flop song from my childhood that sounded best loud. I settled back on the bed, closed my eyes and pressed my thumbs on the lids until I could see pretty patterns wherever I looked.

Alex appeared in a door, towel tied at the waist. Like his face, his chest was cluttered with freckles. Dripping wet it looked like polished stone, some sort of granite to be exact. I thought of a sculpture I'd seen at the city museum. *Untitled Two* was gigantic and so brightly lit all I'd seen was the glare on its surface. Alex was like that.

"Sparks?!" He punched off the radio, then plucked his joint from my lips. Without great music to structure my thoughts everything in the room became very abstract, not just the ideas but the objects. The world of George was one minuscule speck in that constellation. It was light brown and set next to a promi-nent cheekbone. A sarcastic voice boomed from deep inside it. "Cliff, you still with us?"

"Sort of." I shook my head when Alex held out the joint. I felt—I searched for an adequate word—weird. I had to wake up. "Hey, listen," I said, "is there any hot water left?" He grabbed my wrist, yanked me up to my feet and literally pushed me out into the hall. "Come back a new man!" I couldn't tell if he meant it or not.

I stood in the shower. I saw myself as a waterfall. Hot jet streams pounded my head, splashed my shoulders and upper chest, streaked down my ribs, made my pubic hair droop, spilled off the tip of my cock, exploded around my feet. I watched this chain of events for a half hour, struck by how worn out my thinking was.

I wrapped myself in a towel. When I got back to his room Alex eyed me suspiciously. "I said come back a *nude* man." I was supposed to quip, "You wish"—my usual epithet—but I decided against it. I don't know why, and this left a small hole in our afternoon. He realized I had caught him at something. I understood what that was but I wasn't sure whether he knew that I knew or not.

He plopped on the end of the bed, reached out, fiddled with the TV. I knew he was hot for my body. I'd been avoiding the issue for months. Why had I tiptoed around what he couldn't say? We were so much alike mentally. Surely our bodies would match. I closed my eyes and imagined us making out, then stole a glance at my towel. "Guess not," I decided.

As a test I imagined a similar scene with George. I locked us in an embrace. But before I could fasten the lips our bodies started to move by themselves. It had the look of ballet, at least the one I'd been dragged to. I was so wowed by my own choreography I might have whipped out my cock if a lump in my throat hadn't woken me up.

I parted my eyes. I saw a pretty actress in a fake-looking bathroom. Her mouth was open inhumanly wide. Her glazed eyes stared at a mirror. It reflected her screaming face and, further back, the burly chest of a beast with a leather hood over its head. It yanked a bloody axe out of her back and was wiping it off on the front of its T-shirt.

They were replaced by a bottle of Windex. Alex glanced over his shoulder. His face was mildly amused again. "This thing is great," he said. It was his kind of film. It tried to make light of death, made it superficial and sort of witty and, therefore, "great." Thanks to his lecturing I'd come around as well. "Yeah," I agreed, "the day's looking up."

He changed positions. His eyes came so close to mine I was sure I could have seen an emotion in them if one was back there. They were pea green with yellow flecks that looked like tiny dry leaves floating slowly around in bowls of soup. "Neat as a pin," I thought. Or, as Alex liked to explain how he saw the world, "Tears are beside the point."

"Yes, may I help you?" "Oh," I gulped, shifting my gaze to the wall. "I was just spacing out." Being overly stoned was the perfect excuse. He gave me one of his skeptical glares but I wouldn't be tripped up. I even asked for a hit off the joint. "Okay, I guess I believe you," he snapped, and snatched the *TV Guide* off his alarm clock.

"*Young Blood Runs Wild,*" he read aloud. "Three adventurous teenaged couples face horror and death at the hands of a half-human monster." As he spoke, a handsome boy on the TV was pointing his flashlight beam into a cobwebbed room. It found dusty books, a gruesome painting of lapdogs, chairs, an overturned table . . . The jazzy soundtrack swelled up as the murdered girl's face reappeared. His mouth opened inhumanly wide. The hooded beast bounded out of a closet.

He struck it over the head with his flashlight. It hit the floor. He staggered into the hall yelling, "I've killed it. Bobby? Jill?"

They huddled down in a corner. "Come on, I'll show you," their hero said. "No way," Jill gasped, clutching Bobby's hand. But the brave boy ran ahead, gesturing into the death chamber. "See?"

A hairy arm dragged him away. I heard a scream, several yelps, then a gurgling noise. "That must be the air wheezing out of his chopped-open lungs," Alex mumbled. "Let's hope," I joked. The stunned couple eased through the hall and peered into the dark. Their handsome pal was facedown with an axe sticking out of his haircut. "That's it?" Alex groaned. "I'd have *totaled* him."

"Huh?" I was daydreaming. I saw the glare on a windowpane and, framed inside, a sharper take of the shot we'd been glued to. George lay facedown in a living room. A guy with leathery skin was pretending to finish him off. I was transfixed. Then the actors did something so frightening, I jerked my head to the left.

My favorite porn stars were slim, pale teenagers with shoulder-length hair, preferably black. Take the boy sandwiched between two musclemen in the magazine Alex had shoved at me. He had thin skin, shapely legs, a dated haircut and oversized eyes. Best of all, he had one of those asses that open unusually wide.

"Check out this page," Alex said. The star had shoved his ass right in the camera lens. What I'd thought pert at a distance was spooky close up. "No matter how many times I see one of these," Alex leered, "it's still a shock. I mean, as hard as I try I can't look at this thing and recall the boy's face, even though I just told you how hot he is."

True enough, I also couldn't remember its owner. It seemed to have a hypnotic effect. I thought of aliens in sci-fi films who, catching humans' eyes, could wipe our memories clear. This boy's backside wasn't too far removed in appearance from one of those cheaply made monster masks. "Weird, Alex. You're right, as always."

"Let's jerk off," he whispered. We did that sometimes, each holding one edge of a magazine, handling our cocks with the other. I didn't enjoy it as much as my friend, but I did feel a certain thrill knowing how badly he wanted to turn on his side and have sex with me. "Let's share a joint first," I stalled. While he fixed us a fat one I skipped through the small world in front of me.

Page eight: the two musclemen kiss, the boy kneeling in front of them, both cocks between his teeth. Page twenty-two: come dribbling down the boy's chin. Page three: the men sixty-nine. Page eighteen: two cocks inside the boy's ass, his face grimacing. I was admiring the layout when Alex entered my line of sight.

"Does he remind you of George?" he said. "I ask because I can see the resemblance but I think this kid's really hot whereas I'm not attracted to George at all. Here." I took the joint. I was surprised—not that he'd claimed to be wild for George. I just assumed my friend's beauty was one of the world's universals. "Yeah?"

"Sure. I mean, I'll admit George is cute, although cutesy's more like it. He reminds me of a cartoon character. You know, the 'real boy' Pinocchio's forced to become in the old Disney film? Ugh. That's why I still can't imagine the scene you described last night. George's, uh, shit is supposed to be heavy, I guess, but to me the concept is incredibly lightweight."

Maybe it was the grass but I didn't know what he was talking about. I knew George wasn't the star's spitting image. This face was hot whereas George's was so pretty it seemed the work of a plastic surgeon. Maybe George's face gave away too much too soon, but his big saving grace was his strange combination of idealized looks and whatever they bottled up.

I explained this to Alex. "Look," he sighed, "you can't be objective. You're backstage. I'm talking about *presentation*. Let's say our world is a stage, okay? If you buy that, George is a character actor at best, not a sex symbol. Knowing you're hot for him is semi-interesting but, you'll admit this, they'll never base *Gone with the Wind, Part II* on it."

"Well, even so, it's a monument to old-world values in other ways," I said, sounding as vague as I could. I was embarrassed to use the word "love" around Alex, even ironically. He'd just guffaw. "Oh, believe me, I know," he smirked. "Just make sure to keep Winnie-the-Pooh on *your* side of the bed." I slugged his arm and we settled down, magazine propped on our chests.

We agreed on a page where the boy's upper half was in soft focus. Ass filled up most of the frame. The musclemen each held a big, creamy cheek. They grinned happily from either side of the page, like they'd just won a loving cup. I loved the mixture of thoughts in their matching eyes: lust, greed, pride, boredom, and maybe two or three others that didn't matter so much.

Alex unzipped his jeans, which made the usual sputtering noise. I heard a crack as his head turned. I smiled and met his eyes. I just assumed he had noticed how much we resembled the men in the picture. Instead his face looked extremely confused, about to burst into tears or bawl me out. It made me think of the story a friend told me once.

When Joyce was young her family lived in a run-down apartment. Their landlord bragged that his collie could talk. One day it trotted inside at the man's heels. When the landlord said, "Greet the Benairs, Maxwell," it tried to mimic his voice.

Obviously its mouth and jaws weren't built for speech, but it managed to slowly pronounce, in a horrific voice, "I . . . love . . . you."

Alex was like that. I couldn't imagine him mouthing the obvious: "I want to fuck with you, Cliff," or however he might have rephrased that. I realized it was up to me and, looking down at my hard-on, I thought, "Why not see what it means to be hot for a night?" I closed my eyes and unfastened the front of my towel. The porn star's ass clattered onto the floor and flipped shut.

The result was too clumsy for my taste. We re-created a few poses we'd seen in magazines and spent far more time giggling than moaning each other's names. I thought of it as a sort of misplacement, kept George in mind and went right through the motions. I even gave my friend's ass a few superficially passionate strokes to make him think I hadn't tried to forget him.

We came and sat a few feet apart. "Well," Alex said between breaths, "don't you think we've confirmed our big theory that porn is a blueprint for sex? I mean, we look at a photograph and get aroused, yet we still have our wits. But just now I became so distracted by what you were doing to me, I totally lost my perspective."

Driving home, I debated for three seconds and made a sharp turn. George's house was lit up like a storefront, so I rang the bell. His dad, a more wasted George on a much grander scale, pointed down a short corridor. "I think you'll find what you're seeking behind that locked door." We shared a nervous smile, then he went back to his coffee cup.

The hall was lined with family portraits that chronicled the enlargement of George. The story line was okay but the pictures were blurry. The older their dates, the cuter George grew. In '82 he'd looked girlish. In one snapped when he couldn't walk I'd have sworn his dad was kissing a doll's cheek.

"Oh, it's just you," George said. "Quick, come in." He double-bolted the door. The room was crammed with memorabilia, mostly from Disneyland. Everywhere I looked I saw a corny sketch grinning at me. George dashed from wall to wall pointing out characters he liked the best. "Then over here's where I keep the attractions," he said, indicating a handmade altar that must have once been a desk.

He'd stapled photos of each of the famous amusement park's rides on its sides and filled the shelves with scale models of his particular favorites. ". . . The Haunted Mansion, Enchanted Tiki Room, Peter Pan, Space Mountain . . ." He came to the centerpiece, a battered Mickey Mouse cap. He raised the lid ceremoniously. "Here," he said, "is where I keep my acid. Want some?"

I shook my head. "Well, then . . ." He grabbed what I guessed was his diary and a small silver key about the size of a teardrop. ". . . Mind if I finish this?" I found a sittable spot on the floor and watched him write away. His eyes were wider than I'd ever seen them. His room was so dazzling it made the rest of the world seem as dull as a parking lot.

I thought of my bedroom. It was extremely plain: table, chairs, twin bed and sometimes a poster of someone cute. The closest I'd come to creating a niche for myself was a musty storeroom in our basement. Dad kept it locked but one day years ago I'd broken in. Every few months to this day I'd creep down, stretch myself out on the cold cement floor and jerk off.

Maybe that explained why, though surrounded by icons, my mind was filled with pornographic ideas. I imagined George floating facedown in the billows of his double bed. I felt my throat clogging up. I never would have believed I'd think of Alex at an emotional moment but, as tears threatened, I calmed myself by upgrading our time in the sack. At least I'd touched human flesh, even if my aim was off.

"I'm all yours," George said, clicking shut the tiny lock on his red leather booklet. He saw me eyeing it curiously. "Oh, this is where I hide my feelings. In here they don't get in anyone's way." While he buried it under his mattress I wondered how many times my name appeared in the scribbles. "Being articulate wears me out," he yawned, slapping himself in the face.

No kidding. Shortly thereafter his sentences shortened, then I was left asking dumb questions to which he'd shrug, nod or shake his head. During one particularly silent stretch I suggested a walk. "Huh? Oh, right," he shrugged. I followed him out a window. We walked a few blocks very slowly. When we reached a house with a huge front lawn he stopped and stared at it. "Let's sit."

We perched side by side gazing out at the street. Once a big truck roared by carrying some sort of carnival ride on its bed. I'd just decided to ask his opinion when . . . "So," he said softly, "last night." I coughed, then blathered nonstop about how overcome I'd been. First he nodded along, but his eyes grew so glazed that I stopped midapology, raising my eyebrows to mean, "What's wrong?"

"Look at him," I thought. "He's so far away from the way I've felt. I'm sick of treating his moods with kid gloves. I want to figure his body out and get him over with, if it comes down to that. He won't know the difference, and, whatever happens, at least I'll stop feeling this tense. Okay, do it."

"Let's go back." There was a flicker of warmth in his eyes. I helped him up to his feet. In the dark between streetlights my thoughts raced. When a yellowy glow made him visible I reaffirmed what I already knew. The walk was lined with magnolia trees. Their strong, ambiguous odor had always repulsed me. Tonight they smelled like my come and I shared that with George. "How would I know?" he whispered.

We climbed back through his window. "Just stretch out here," I said, gesturing toward his bed. As I undressed I glanced around at the walls completely covered with mice, ducks, dogs, crickets and so on. When I squinted they looked like the crowd at a strip joint. If life were a sketch, I was sure I'd be deafened by high-pitched yells of encouragement.

I carefully re-created what I had seen through Philippe's window, up to the point when I'd felt nauseous. I was a little too tentative but George's lack of response made it seem we'd rehearsed our parts hundreds of times. I left my come somewhere deep in his back. I was surprised by how coldly he watched me get dressed, but I decided to not think until we were miles apart.

The further I drove, the more our sex mattered. George was a slight worry but, as I started to think how amused friends would be by the more bizarre aspects, he took a backseat. By the time I'd reached my house and dialed the only phone number I knew by heart, he was less of an issue. I thought the ringing would never stop. Then I heard a familiar voice. "Alex," I said. "Get this."

ALEX

THE REPLACEMENTS

Alex, 17, is slouched in an old movie theater chatting with friends. Lights dim. He peeks at Cliff's crotch. As *Explosives* begins—damaged print—he feels torn between what he's observing—four wrestling hippies—and a sweet daydream—Cliff fucking him violently on a twin bed. The scenes get mixed up in his mind, like images in those light shows that stoned hippies used to project over rock concerts back in the late sixties. Alex pretends he's on acid. After a minute or two, the sex slowly dissolves in his eyesight.

He watches one star topple back, hit his head on a rock and stop moving. The hippies untangle. One puts his ear to the

victim's chest, stares, shakes his head. Alex's cock is still hard
from his fantasy. The actor playing the dead boy has freckles.
Alex imagines his friends lug him into an alley, undress the
corpse, then themselves, and gang-bang him. In truth the stars
call for help, but the truth has already dissolved in this fantasy.

When the corpse has been sapped by his former chums, and
their inventive if dated invectives thin, Alex blinks. His cock
deflates. A funeral is in progress. Some bad actors bawl, stag-
ger, screech. The freckled boy lies in a box on a flower-strewn
mound of dirt. "No," Alex thinks, "reputation or not, this
film's a yawn, however startling it might have been in the
sixties. The corpse would be thirty by now and the world's
grown more hellish. A baby could see this and not feel the
slightest bit dazed by its moral."

Alex turns to Cliff. "You want to leave?" Cliff's eyes say no.
Alex fights a desire to be fucked on the floor, then attempts to
rejoin the film. "What's Cliff seeing in it?" he wonders, shifting
his gaze back and forth from his friend to the huge square of
images. Three hippies kick a Coke can down a road. Cliff's eye
movements don't match the actions on-screen. Maybe it isn't the
film he's enjoying, but some private story. Alex acquires an
intense need to know, then this longing dissolves in more perti-
nent thoughts.

For Alex life is a series of gradual dissolves—one thought or
mood or companion dissolving into another, over and over. It's a
term he hears bandied about in his evening film workshop. The
teacher will show classic artifacts—*M, Potemkin, The Blue
Angel*—take a few steps to the right of the screen and subdivide
what the long-dead directors meant. As an experiment, Alex
has tried to apply this idea to his life, remaining just to the side
of whatever is taking place and narrating its course as though he
were the voice of a rather pretentious spy story.

The actors enter a hippie nightclub. They buy two beers. Cut to the bartender's face concentrating on pouring their drinks into glasses. Alex would like to poke Cliff and explain how the film's tempo makes this switch possible without disturbing its slight credibility, but Cliff would stare, shake his head and not know what that meant. He's too easily swept up by surface activity, rushed from one view to another, his blue-green eyes glazed, his mouth deformed by a meaningless smile. Hypothetically, Cliff would be distant-acquaintance material. In person, Alex cannot take his eyes off the guy.

Alex shoots Cliff a glance. "So, imagine the guy's a total stranger," he thinks. "What's my knee-jerk reaction?" He narrows his feelings to lust and disinterest. "Fine, where do they spring from?" Cliff's face. "What about it?" The way its mysterious beauty dissolves when George Miles is the topic. George provides content where Alex would rather hallucinate freely. Two-thirds of his weekly allowance is spent buying drugs to undermine George's spell. After a joint or two George disappears to a certain extent, and Cliff's eyes sport a flexible stare again.

Alex's thoughts trail off. The film attracts them. Its hippie actors have formed a collective of some sort. They march down a quaint main street carrying signs with dumb slogans and crudely drawn peace symbols. But in the meantime, their dads have formed a gang of their own, wielding shotguns. Before the young stars can change the world they're sent to prison. Alex peers over at Cliff, who is lost in a daydream. His pupils aren't even bouncing around anymore. They sit perfectly still, pointed down, and look vaguely wet. "George," Alex sneers to himself.

Dissolve. Alex is thinking about the relationship between his life and film's version of "life." At first his thoughts are too scattered, then they gravitate to the project he's soon to embark on. As part of his evening class he must direct a short film. It's a requirement, as well as a good chance to focus his thoughts, which are weak in the story line area. His fascination with Cliff, sex and violence suggests a kind of sixties-styled light show transposed to the present. He's juggling lots of ideas: porn scenario, B-movie parody, rock opera, pseudosnuff, others.

They need a center, a theory, a sense of belief. He believes in the power of film to sanitize the unthinkable. But such a cross-hatch must seem to reflect one clear viewpoint, and Alex feels very divided, as though his self and his self-understanding were merely atop one another with no sense of how they might coalesce, much less attract an audience. This needs intense thought. Luckily, the boring film is dissolving at last. The boys and their fathers relax in the nightclub seen earlier, sipping tea. The End, it says. The words obscure them. Alex turns to Cliff. "I'm going."

Alex rolls onto his back and bends his knees, encircling them with one arm until the crack in his ass widens and lifts a foot off the bed. The rest is up to whoever. He didn't catch the guy's name. In fact he's wondering if his decision to go home with blondie was logical. He'd had a few drinks on the guy's tab. The bar was peculiarly empty. He'd been amazed by the sound of The Jesus and Mary Chain, a covert pop group, mixed in with the flightier disco. *Something* transported him here, ripped his shirt trying to take it off. He watches the face he'd been grinning at all evening eat out his crack as though it were a scene in a porn tape he's renting.

If that were the case he could judge his sex partner more clearly. As is, he's too distracted by personal traits and sketchy fragments of history. They came out over drinks and remain an issue now, when everything but good looks should be pointless.

Alex knows, for example, that blondie's attracted to freckles because they remind him of pennies strewn inside a wishing pond, his favorite memory of childhood. He fixates on asses because they're so rounded and pondlike. Slobbering over them seems to refill his more dried-up emotions, or something like that.

For Alex's part, he has always felt very detached from his freckles. When strangers make a big deal out of them it just confuses him. What's he supposed to say? Skin's skin. What's the point of decoding it? Freckles aren't painful. They don't crackle when touched, as dry leaves would do. They're not reminders of anything, like scars. This blond's fascination with them has no bearing on him. Occasionally a tongue disappears up his asshole and he feels involved, though it's still kind of vague, like he's passing the scene of a crime and gets hit by a stray bullet.

He picks up one of the blond guy's porn novels, which they'd been perusing to get in the mood. It's called *Chicken Lickin'*. The cover art is an incompetent sketch of a boy on his hands and knees, bracketed by two distorted men. One has his hand in the shape of a gun and is pointing it at the boy's ass-crack. The other man aims his cock at the boy's mouth, which grins or grimaces. The men are absurdities: arms too long, cocks like cannons, hands withered. The chicken's malformed as well, buttocks overinflated, his eyes reminiscent of bullet holes.

Alex opens the book and reads a passage at random. "Toby's ass was public property. Whitey looked hard down its steaming tube. 'He may be young,' Whitey hissed, 'but he's got a real hellhole.' Pedro stroked his colossal dong. 'Hot mouth too,' Whitey added. 'Hot stuff at both ends.' A line of spittle ran down his chin. 'And good enough to be eaten, I'd say,' he winked, shoving his face between Toby's soft ass-mounds. 'Eat me,' Toby cried huskily. 'Clean it, you fucker.' As Toby spoke his pit slowly relaxed. Whitey gulped down its dark, hidden fruit."

"I would pick that page." Alex tenses a bit at the memory of Cliff's boyfriend George in the same situation. In fact, at three steps removed—first enacted by strangers behind glass, then filtered out through his friend's vague account, then overlaid with wretched prose—the scene that embarrassed him during Cliff's story seems much more intriguing, a fiction dissolved of allusion. Alex's eyes, which have narrowed in irony, flit to the drama between his legs. As an experiment, he tries to master the tone of the novel, in order to silently ornament his experience.

"The blond stud pushed harder with his darting tongue— that's ridiculous—curling the rough muscle into a pointed tool that pushed my sphincter—ugh—forcing it, uh . . . to relax as my tight ass-mouth opened—that's awful—accepting the stud's wet caresses with a proud . . . lunge, I guess. It was, uh, marked by a cry of relief from my . . . parched lips . . . let's see, a whimpered sigh of surrender as my whole body relaxed, gladly taking this anal intrusion—shit—hungrily ready for more, ready to . . . to . . . take this blond hunk in any . . . shit . . ." Alex stops for a second. "I have to do better than that. Okay . . .

"The blond wormed his tongue up my shit-chute. That's better. 'I've struck gold,' he said in a . . . muffled voice . . . uh, swallowing thick . . . wads of ass-tinged saliva. Good. 'You're hot, really hot,' he continued, addressing my . . . gleaming hills. Mmm. He stroked his hard-on so roughly he could have been . . . signing his name on a contract. That's funny. My pink butthole widened with each probing . . . lunge of his lick muscle, until the hole was humongous and . . . and . . . rubbery. God. 'Say ah,' I moaned. God. He did. Then I loaded his mouth with my rancid brown . . . unh . . ."

Alex has managed to come and, by so doing, seem half-involved in the sex, but his calves ache. "That wasn't bad," he says, wriggling free and standing up in one motion, then reconvening his clothes. "Enigmatic, not too complex, quick." He smiles down at his partner and finds the blond rubbing his eyes, either tired or disconsolate. "I really hate it when people use words to describe an emotion," the blond sniffs, then sobs quietly. Alex wipes come on a handful of Kleenex and steps through the wobbly holes in his shorts. "Mind if I take this?" He picks up the novel.

"Look," he continues, "we used each other. It's over. You've got things to do. I've got things to do. Period." That does the trick. The blond tumbles onto his stomach, shoves his face in a pillow and kicks his lower legs, swimming-instructor-style. Alex is barely involved in the formalities of dressing, chatting, waving goodbye. His experiment with the pornography haunts him. Its tone and his eyesight have merged like his film teacher's knowledge of plot seems to do with a weathered print. Somewhere amidst this consolidation is a great work of art. "I can't picture it," he mutters. "I need a blank wall." He fumbles around for his car keys.

He lies in bed, notebook propped on his lap, scribbling. Spread around him are various magazines, open to pictures of muscular bodies stripped nude, roughly fastened together. Running alongside each shot is an X-rated story line, added on later, that tries to explain their disjointedness as violent, mutual hunger. But Alex knows they're actors. What the text presupposes has no more connection with them than they have with each other. It's these gaps that Alex keeps glancing at. They're what his scrawl is about.

Alex enters his math class and picks a clean seat. The teacher writes giant numbers across the front blackboard. Students open their notebooks and copy them down. One, a boy sitting two seats to Alex's left, is excessively pretty. "He should be a chipmunk," Alex decides, leaning forward to scrutinize. Draw a few rings round the eyes, dye his hair, make him lose a few pounds and he could be George Miles on a good day. "Well, close enough," Alex thinks, lowering pen to page. He scratches wildly, stops, studies his stuntman, then blackens some more of the notepaper.

"George made men's mouths water. 'And I know why,' the boy muttered. He snuggled low in the couch, grabbed his legs and raised them high in the air, so his pants grew real tight to his ass. It stuck out like the prow of a pirate ship. Drool dribbled over Cliff's chin. 'I just knew it,' George thought. 'I'm gonna give him a taste.' He bent his knees, which ripped the seat of his pants open. Cliff was there in a flash. He completed the job, shoved his face through the frayed cloth. 'Here it comes, babe,' George grunted. 'Unh!' "

Alex runs out of ideas. He shakes his head to dissolve the absurd voice. His stuntman comes into focus. The boy tilts sideways in his chair, trying to suss out what Alex was writing. The boy squints for a while, then gives up and casts curious looks in his schoolmate's direction for the rest of the class. When the bell rings he gathers his books and strolls over. "I'm David," he smiles, sticks his hand out. "I know," Alex says, "you're the retard who thinks he's a pop star." The boy's hand withdraws. "These are notes for a porn film. You want to be in it?" The boy stiffens. Something tells him to walk away. He gets lost.

Alex is hustling down the hall, notebook spread out like a map across his arms, rereading his porn, when he notices George Miles a few yards ahead. The kid's scrawny ass does its limited trick, jiggling slightly. Thanks to Cliff, Alex can't see it without getting jealous. He quickens his pace. "Hey, Miles," he says, "got a sec?" They retreat to a small square of grass in the heart of the school buildings. "I'm directing a film and I want you to star in it." George is apparently too stoned to comprehend. "Cliff plays your lover and"—Alex debates for a moment—"he eats your, uh, shit."

He has managed to animate George's face, but its expression lacks depth. He starts again with the addition of several provocative details, the thrust of which—payment in drugs—evokes the needed response. George clears his throat. "Cliff's my lover?" When Alex nods, the boy's grin makes him seem almost human. "You said a film? Sure, when, what drugs?" Five minutes later, Alex is strolling away toward the school cafeteria, a little vacant with happiness. With George as bait, Cliff is sure to see worth in the project.

He fills his tray with a sandwich, some french fries, an Orange Crush, then walks through the long, crowded tables. There's Cliff's handsome face chewing something up. Alex imagines its mouth smeared with shit, and his cock hardens. "Christ," he thinks, "I'd better cool myself off." He tries to picture a vast crowd of startled film critics. That doesn't help, but his blue jeans are fairly loose. "Hi, pal." He sits and announces his project's beginnings, allows himself to be slapped on the back, then pops the question. "No," Cliff says.

Alex rephrases the question several times. Each time Cliff makes up a different excuse. Although the excuses are standard—disgust, guilt, embarrassment, decency—all of them somewhat negotiable, they obviously hide a more boring concern. "You're still in love with that twerp," Alex crows. "No," Cliff responds. "That's the past. But there *was* something there and you're making it . . ." Alex's thoughts trail off. He must decide how to salvage his project. He forces a smile, wanders into his gym class, and goes through the motions of hitting a baseball.

"You're out!" Alex plops on the bench between someone he knows well enough to say hi to and someone he hates. He watches the pitcher's grand style of delivery, then the bored outfielders shouting things back and forth, then the immense chain link fence that circumscribes the campus. Just beyond, walking slowly along some parked cars, is a former A student, expelled for possession of drugs. Alex had sex with his brother once. Its nuts and bolts were disastrous. Kenneth looked so frail that Alex was scared he would break something. Still, four months later when Kenneth had dropped dead from some kind of brain cancer, Alex was glad he'd gone through with it. Rrrrring.

"Hey, genius." Cliff rushes his way through a crowded hall. "I've got a thought," Cliff continues, wrapping one arm around Alex's neck. They veer toward the shade of an elm tree. "Why don't you shoot the real thing, through Philippe's window? It's up your alley. Besides, you could art it up in the editing room or whatever you call it." Alex yawns. "I'll even show you the place, be your cinematographer." Alex nods, yawns. When he yawns his mouth opens extremely wide. Someone once told him it looks like he's crying wolf.

He walks Cliff to biology class. As they chat, the film assembles itself before Alex's eyes. Cliff's particularly sharp, or some drug has inspired him. He talks about fucking George in such blasé, edgy terms that he could be describing the plot of a porn magazine. Once they get to the crossroads there's quite a rapport. Alex stops dead. "When we finish the shooting tonight, let's fuck," he says. Cliff keeps walking. When he's a few yards ahead he shrugs. "I'll take that as a yes," Alex yells. "Thanks!" He runs to astronomy.

* * *

Alex creeps through the foliage. "Sssh," says a voice just behind him. "Straight on past the . . . Yeah, just a foot or two further . . . You're there. I'll be back at the car." Alex gets to his feet. As Cliff explained there's a neat little space between bushes and window where he can stand comfortably, kept dark by the crest of damp leaves overhead. He fiddles around with his light meter. The room is nightmarishly lit. He plugs one eye and frames the black-and-white furnishings within the fractured square etched on the lens. Philippe and George perch on facing chairs, five, maybe six feet apart. He can just fit them in.

George's body is nothing apart from his crotch, which resembles a mouse. His head sways on top of that vague streak of whiteness, a kitsch souvenir, its lips and eyes the unnatural colors of candies. Alex pans to Philippe. "Too much skull," he thinks. "It really swallows the face." What few details there are seem generically French—sharp featured, unshaven. From the neck down he's fat, and to Alex all fat is identical. "I'll try to improvise now, and write the real porn stuff later." He uses the lens as a monocle while the kid takes a few tipsy steps and collapses facedown on the carpet. "Okay, well . . .

"He eyed George's ass. It lay in front of his chair like a footstool. 'That's gotta be the worst piece of flesh I've ever seen,' he thought. Drool dribbled down his chin. 'Jesus, you'd think I was starving to death.' He almost laughed at himself. He stuck out his foot and kicked it. 'The fucker's real enough.' He started wiping one hand back and forth on his big, veiny cock. 'Listen, baby,' he said. 'Keep your mouth shut.' He planted one foot on each buttock and pushed the crack open, licking his lips at the hairless pink slit. 'You could mount that thing on a ring,' he joked.

"He knelt down, reached behind him and found a small flashlight. He parted the ass-crack and aimed a bright beam at the red cavern. 'You're pointless,' he growled, looking over its glossy walls. 'I need a snoutful.' He did a sharp nosedive and smelled something rancid but rich, like the trace of perfume in a king's tomb. He flattened his face on the butt, sucked and chewed at the hole, but his treasure was stuck in its vault. He introduced a few fingers. They twisted the tube in an interesting way, but not wildly enough.

" 'Fine, have it your way,' he said. '*Don't* give me what I want, but you'll be sorry, kid.' He started slapping the ass with ferocity. He laughed out loud as the pert globes turned purple and twitched into ugly shapes. 'This'll teach you to mess with me,' he thought. The skimpy body was tossing around like a beached fish. The sight made his prick leak. 'I've landed the boy of the century,' he thought. 'No shit. Man, those sunken eyes, that runny nose, those chapped lips.' He gave his hand a rest.

" 'You get my point?' he said firmly. 'I want the goods, George. A lovely thing like you shouldn't have some ugly junk up your ass. I'll take it off your hands. Get me?' The stud poised his face by the glowering mounds. A prize emerged, ripe and hot from its bowel oven. He caught the brown morsel between his teeth. Whipping his fierce, swordlike prong into a frenzy, he gulped the abhorrent meal down in one bite. 'Just like Mom used to make,' he sneered.

"As a reward for the youngster's behavior, Philippe gave the ass a quick tongue bath. 'Good as new,' he surmised with a wink. 'Now let's complete the job.' He fit the huge, sopping head of his love muscle to George's pucker and worked the entire seven inches inside. 'Oh, you're the loosest one ever,' he groaned. Arching his hips, cock touched bottom. When he withdrew, it was covered with crumbs. 'Fuck, fuck, fuck,' Philippe chanted, increasing his tempo. 'You're gross!' And it wasn't too long before gobs of come plummeted into the wimp with a noisy splash. Cut."

When Alex gets back to the car Cliff has locked its doors and gone to sleep in the back seat. He bangs on a window. Cliff lurches up, slurs some words. They sound like, "So, what did you think?" "Banal," Alex says, starting the car. "Even as porn, there's so little to work with. For all the mystique of the shit, Phillipe's sex has a regimentation, as if it's been too well thought out, or performed once too often. At this point, it's all in the telling. . . ." Cliff's snores interrupt him. He drives off, turns left down a street lined with huge, ostentatious homes.

It's late, so they've blended together. Only their top floors, in one or two cases, are still lit, like watchtowers. Suddenly there is a very dark stretch in the row on the right. He puts his foot on the brake, rolls his window down. Legend has it this house has been empty for decades, since a depressed father killed his two kids there. No one will touch it. Occasionally lunatics claim they've seen transparent children run into the street like they're chasing a ball. Alex has long-standing dreams to use its grounds for a big-budget splatter film.

Sometimes he drives here alone, parks, and sits on the curb for a couple of hours, taking notes. The basic line he's come up with has three or four drunk teenaged boys sneaking into the place. A psychotic, deformed guy is using the house for his hideout. He spots the intruders, makes chase, rapes and murders them one by one. It's a conventional plot, but the rapes make it fresh. At the moment he's too tired to do more than stare at the gate. Once he gets bored with that, he turns to see what position Cliff's sleeping in.

"Home!" he commands himself. The road is straight but looks tapered, a shiny sword aimed at his neighborhood. When he's exhausted, he's prone to seeing daydreamy mirages out there on the route. Since his thoughts are a mess, it's a real sixties light show. He tries to separate Cliff from Philippe from himself from George, the sexy parts from the dreck, and at the same time keep just between two white lines. When a truck pulls in front of him, he's far too busy to notice. When he does, he puts his foot on the brake a half second too late.

Alex is slumped in his wheelchair. "I was asleep for a week. When I woke up I . . ." He lifts the front of his T-shirt. Using a finger, he draws a jagged line across his stomach. "Below that's the vulture meat," he says. "Go ahead, kick it or shoot it or something." Cliff reaches out, pokes his friend's knee. "Zilch," Alex sneers. "I'm a seat pad. My nephew was visiting yesterday and he climbed into my lap and said, 'You're pretty comfortable.' " Just then a teenaged boy screams from the TV. It draws their attention. A shadowy figure is stabbing him over and over. "That's the worst look of terror I've ever seen," Alex says.

"I've been okay," Cliff mumbles. Alex turns, startled. "What? Oh, right, I heard. Spotless." He knows he should look at Cliff, but his eyes naturally flit to the TV instead. Long dead, the teenager is still being hacked. To simulate blood, a red light has been trained on the body. It can't hide the trick knife, whose blade recedes into the handle with each thrust. "Either these films are becoming more shoddily made," Alex groans, "or my eyesight's improving." He takes a big hit off his joint and hands it over to Cliff.

The shadowy figure slips out the door of what looks like a haunted house, inching along an old canopied porch toward a window. Five boys are standing inside. "Don't ask me, man," one says. "I didn't *ask* you, I *told* you, Bob." "Alex, I feel sort of guilty. My not being hurt, I mean." "What? Oh, don't worry," Alex smiles, watching the shadow observe the young actors. "At least I don't feel like castrating your boyfriends. Plus, this film, it just . . . absorbs me." Glass breaks. The shadow yanks at an actor, then severs his head on the splintering pane. The gore is replaced by a girl's face.

"When you chew gum, chew the best. . . ." Alex rolls to the TV and turns down the volume. "Don't worry," he says, "I'm more advanced now. Remember those creatures in *Star Trek* who'd gradually evolved over millions of years into gigantic brains floating deep in space?" He lifts his shirt, points to some freckles. "Look hard, you might see Orion." Cliff snorts, but his eyes remain wary or quizzical. "Hmm," Alex adds, "I know, I'll read your mind." He feigns a sort of religious trance, eyes rolled back in his head, fingers pressed to his temples. "What has become of your film, right?"

Cliff nods sheepishly. "Wait fifteen minutes," Alex says. "This stupid thing's almost over." He cranks up the volume, withdraws a few feet from the set. Boys are scampering everywhere. One pixieish kid, who has spent the film cracking bad jokes in a bid for the other guys' sympathy, hides in a closet. "I'm fine," he gasps, sinking down to the floor. "Mom, Dad, you won't believe this . . ." Alex tenses. He pictures the skin being torn off the kid and gobbled down like a pancake. The closet door shatters. A knife cuts the kid's throat in close-up. "Gee, thanks," he gurgles.

Alex wheels to the TV again, grabs his *Guide* and finds the listing. "We've still got another half hour to go," he groans. "No way." He turns down the volume and faces Cliff. "So, you weren't hurt at all. That's great. I mean, I can hardly imagine your hot body squishing all over the place. No, God's choosy. Here, have a joint." Cliff catches it. "You don't look so bad," he says. "Give me a year," Alex grins, "I'll settle." He lowers his eyes to Cliff's crotch, which produces a tingle in his upper half. It feels like a prickly shirt.

He points at a gray film can lying on top of his Sonic Youth bootleg LP. "It's finished. My dad drove me down to the lab and I sliced a few awkward transitions." Cliff clears his throat. "Well, the porn narration, how . . . ?" "Oh, that was simple, like fishing probably is. I sat at my desk and thought of what I'd dreamt up at the window. My arm started jerking, and suddenly there was this primitive thing on the table. In fact"—he creaks up to his desk, pulls drawers open, removes a file folder— "maybe you'd read this to make sure it's sexy. I checked it against some porn and they appeared to match."

He watches Cliff squint at his handwriting. He has that prickly shirt on again. He's imagining them in bed now, here, tonight. He rearranges their bodies until something works. He thinks of that film *Coming Home* where Jon Voight played a paralyzed Vietnam vet who had sex with Jane Fonda. He's sure both their faces were sweaty and creased, same as porn stars'. "It's clever," Cliff says. "Making George seem a corpse is inspired, and he does sort of turn into one when you're with him. The night we fucked I had this weird feeling I was alone and not alone at the same time.

"The shit part works because you use the right adjectives. But if I actually saw shit come out of George, I'd still feel nauseous, I think." Alex frowns, considers this, then says, "I used to have a real clear mental picture, but sex, shit, they're not all that different now. Speaking of which . . ." Cliff looks up. "You remember our plan for the ill-fated night?" Cliff averts his eyes. Alex traces his gaze to the face of a dying young actor. A nervous voice, which doesn't sync with the wrenched lips and chattering teeth of the victim, says, "I'll try." Alex smiles at the face.

He directs his old friend through the preparations. First the light switch. Next Cliff removes his own clothes. Alex watches him fold back the bedcovers, ripping them clean from the mattress. Cliff reaches Alex, wraps both arms tightly around his chest and raises him to his feet. Resting his weight on Cliff's shoulder and head, Alex fumbles around with his buttons, snaps, zippers. Cliff carries Alex, half-lifting, half-dragging his heels on the carpet, toward the bed. "Thanks," Alex says, as Cliff straightens him out then rolls him onto his stomach. "Lube's in the drawer."

Sometimes Cliff's hand strokes his back very rapidly, as though attempting to rub out a stain. Alex wonders if he should pretend it's a rape and is beginning to try when Cliff sighs, "I just can't get it hard." Alex considers this, then reaches over and takes a porn magazine off the small stack on his night table, hurling it onto his back. He hears the pages turn. They feel like wings. "Hey, great. I'm *in*." Alex can't tell the difference. He looks at the TV. The shadowy figure lies dead. A handsome actor steps back from the thing, drops his knife and squints into the lens of the camera. The End, it says. The words obscure them.

GEORGE

WEDNESDAY, THURSDAY, FRIDAY

George streaked toward his room. "I'm home." He passed the kitchen door. His dad was drinking espresso. "George, wait . . ." He double-bolted his door. "I know it's here," he thought, pawing through a desk drawer. At the bottom were two crinkled typewritten pages.

They contained detailed descriptions, in French, of how he looked, smelled and tasted. Philippe had presented them to him a few weeks ago, with the words, "This is you in a—how you say?—nutshell." "He should know," George thought. "Now if I buy a French dictionary . . ."

"George?" He dropped the pages and kicked them under his

bed. "Just a second." He let his dad in. "Son, I thought we might go for a drive to the ridge and look down at the pretty lights. How about it?" That was the last thing George wanted to do. "I'm busy." "I just thought . . ." *Really,* Dad."

Mr. Miles wandered back to the kitchen. George lifted his Mickey Mouse cap, grabbed a tab of the acid he'd stashed there, and slipped it under his tongue. He set The Cramps' "Garbage Man" forty-five on his turntable. ". . . *Do you understand? / Do you understand? . . .*" By its end he was seeing things.

There was a huge map of Disneyland over his bed. He liked to stare at it, picture his favorite Lands or imagine new areas stocked with rides. Acid helped. He closed his eyes and, in ten seconds flat, he was tiptoeing through an attraction.

Room after room after room of incredible holograms. Over his head, a Milky Way of skulls snapped like turtles. He was knee-deep in a lime green fog populated by see-through ghosts skimpy as Kleenexes. A booming, vaguely familiar voice wafted out of the camouflaged speakers. "Georges?"

"Shit, what time is it?" He opened his eyes. For a couple of seconds the ride and his bedroom were double-exposed like a photograph. The Goofy clock on his little night table read six thirty-seven. "I'm late," he gasped, shooting up to his feet. "Bye, Dad." He slammed the front door.

He stood on the sidewalk and stuck out his thumb. A trucker chose him. The guy seemed friendly enough, but he kept asking personal questions. "Do you have a girlfriend?" he leered at one point. "Look, I'm on acid, so leave me alone, all right?" That shut him up. George hallucinated in peace.

He knocked. Philippe let him in. "Georges, uh, my friend Tom is here and I thought . . ." "Phil, he's a spectacle." It was an older man. He looked like a stork wearing glasses. "Thanks," George said quickly. "Uh, Tom," Philippe said, "Georges and I will be very alone for a minute."

"I thought a change would be good," he continued, once Tom left the room. George was pissed off, but the acid made anger seem corny to him at that moment. More than anything, he was amazed by Philippe's eyes. They looked unusually pleased, but he felt even less warmth than ever from them.

"Prepare and I will see you back here." George walked to the bathroom, stripped. He stared at the mirror while all sorts of scattered thoughts raced through his mind. None stayed long enough to complete themselves. "Later," he said aloud, popping a zit on his upper back.

He lay facedown on the living room rug. Philippe's friend said some nice things about him. One of the two guys caressed his ass, then used some fingers to open its hole so wide George felt cold air rush in. "Maybe," Tom said, to which Philippe answered, "Good."

How had Philippe put it? "Your asshole looks like a child's pout . . ." George couldn't remember the rest. "Shit, baby." That was Philippe's voice, so George pushed a couple of turds out. "What does he normally eat?" Tom asked. "Hamburgers, french fries, candy bars . . ." "I could have guessed."

Two fingers slid up his ass. Since he'd met Philippe, George had learned how to count them. Two more joined in. He hadn't taken that many before. "Not bad," he thought. Someone felt for his lips, pried them open and four fingers slid down his throat. "He's got a big mouth," Tom whispered, "I love that."

George gagged a few times. "Let it loose," Philippe said in a soothing voice. George didn't want to, then he was vomiting. When that ran out he noticed most of Tom's hand was inside his hole. The other was fiddling around in his throat like it had dropped something.

Someone was spanking him. Picturing how his ass looked usually helped him relax. He knew the thing was bright red, but he couldn't imagine an arm sticking out of it. Maybe it looked like an elephant. If that was so, Tom's praise made more sense. "Really," George thought, "that *would* be great."

"Oh, God, I . . . take this child . . . beyond the . . . shit!" Some of the words were Tom's, some Philippe's. Come splattered over his ass, back and legs. The hands withdrew. "Is there anything else you want to understand?" That was Philippe's voice. "No, got it." Tom.

George sat up. He couldn't see very well, but he picked out Tom's glasses. "Do you have any idea how soft you are inside?" Tom asked. George felt incredibly stoned. He managed to say, "I guess." Philippe laughed. "You must have been fisted before." That was Tom again. "No." George shook his head.

Once George had showered and dressed, Tom gave him a lift. All the way home Tom kept asking if he had enjoyed himself, then if he liked playing dead, then if he'd thought about killing himself. "I'm not sure. Maybe. Not really." "Just between us," Tom said, "if you decide to go all the way, call me. Tom Brathwaite. I'm in the book."

George lay in bed wondering what the guy meant by "all the way." Did that mean Tom would dissuade him, or that he'd assist? George decided to jot down the guy's number, just in case. He tiptoed into the hall, scanned the phone book and crept back to safety.

He looked around at his room. There was the Disneyland map; there the poster of Pluto, his ears flying up in the air; there the Mickey and Minnie desk lamp; there the oval-shaped mirror with Donald Duck chasing his nephews around the frame. He struggled up, took the mirror from its nail.

He laid it out on the floor. He pulled his ass open, hoping to see what the men were so wild about. He could guess it'd resemble a cave, but, with the swelling and stuff, it looked exactly like Injun Joe's Cave, his eighth or ninth favorite Disney-land ride at the moment.

He'd stumbled upon it five years ago. Inside, it was a slight disappointment—too narrow and crowded—but he still made a beeline for it at least once every visit and spent a while outside its painted mouth, squinting into the dark, covered with goose bumps.

He climbed into bed and was almost asleep when he thought of his diary. He hadn't written in it for weeks. Once he'd thought it would empty him out. But writing was no help. It just kept his feelings from getting lost. "Still, why not?"

"Drugs are finally getting to me. I'm going through things I guess I shouldn't because it seems fun, but it isn't. Does that make sense? I don't know anymore, and I don't really care. Life's sort of out of control, though I guess that's my own stupid fault.

"I think the last time I wrote, Cliff and I were best friends. He changed a lot. We wave to each other at school, but that's it. I shouldn't have let him have sex with me. He told me we would be friends for eternity. He said a lot of things. All shit.

"This is so boring. I guess that's why I stopped writing. I'm fucked up. I don't know what to do. I don't even think I'm alive anymore. I'm walking around but I'm not really there. If I didn't have sex with Philippe I'd go nuts.

"School's nothing. I hate my friends. Nobody's interested in me anymore. They think I'm cute then they get really bored. If I don't sleep with people they hate me. But when I do they think they know me or something. I hope not.

"I don't know what I should call Philippe. He doesn't love me, I guess. It's weird he's not getting bored, but that's because he pretends I'm dead. I can't understand what that stuff's all about. But I don't mind. It doesn't matter.

"I've been trying to make myself great for a long time. I know I'm too closed around people, but when I talk, like with Cliff, it doesn't make any difference. I can still be amusing sometimes, except it's more like just weird lately.

"I keep saying I'll change and I want to. But all I do is get tense. That's okay for a while. Acid's great but I think stupid things while I'm on it. I still dream of living in Disneyland. I don't know how long I've been saying that.

"I guess I hope something fantastic is going to happen. I don't think it's up to me. I'll try but it's hard to say stuff like that without getting bored. Like right now I'm totally bored. I don't understand that."

George felt like shit. The clock focused. Seven-twelve. He dressed and ran to the bus stop. His shirt was on inside out. "Shit." He climbed in and sat behind Jerry Cox. George liked to look at the back of his head. His hair was blond, wavy, thick. It made George think of a crystal ball. He planned the day ahead.

At school he hit the head, took some acid. He was hallucinating all morning. Algebra, woodshop and history drifted past, like puffy clouds when he lay on his back. At noon he dumped his textbooks in his locker and filled up a tray in the lunchroom. Paul was waiting for him at their usual table.

After a few minutes Sally and Max, her new boyfriend, joined in. Max told some racist jokes. Sally constructed a tower of Pepsi cans and dubbed it *George Miles Nude*. They shared an angry look. Paul pointed out a drug dealer who sold "the best grass in the universe." George made a mental note.

George was taking his last bite of spice cake when Fred, a

dumb jock, wandered by. "Hey, fag," Fred said as he sauntered by, "I hear you're shit in bed." George pretended he hadn't quite heard that. The asshole always made fun of him.

"George, what . . ." "Forget it, Paul." "What's this about?" Sally piped in. "Something wrong, George?" He tried to play it cool. "No, nothing. It's just some bullshit a former best friend of mine's spreading around." Sally's face whitened. "Gee, I thought *I* was your former best friend." "Jesus," George thought.

Ten minutes later George saw liar David sit down at the next table. He leaned over and yelled, "I hear you're Cliff's latest fuck." David blushed, spilled some milk down his shirt. "Oh, hi. I didn't think you would mind. I admire you a lot." George scowled and left him in peace. "Anyway, Sally . . ."

The bell rang. George waved goodbye. He was heading for chemistry class when he thought he heard, "Hey, Miles." Mr. McGough pinned his head in a vise grip, dragging him into an empty class. "Got any grass, addict?" "No, fucking let me go!" "Oh, such a tough kid," the teacher laughed.

"When are we going to hang out?" George whined. McGough cleared his throat, grinned, "I like you George. You know that. If I were gay . . ." But George knew he was gay. He'd propositioned Paul recently, then thrown a fit when it didn't work out. Next thing Paul knew, there was a giant red *F* on his book report.

There was no point in confronting McGough. He'd never drop his guard. "See ya," George said. "Fuck it," is what he meant. He was a few minutes late for class, but no problem. He poured the blue liquid in with the yellow stuff and brought the goo to a boil. Blub, blub, blub.

$CO^2 + N$ = nitrogen oxide or some such shit. He'd never made sense of any of it. He watched the second hand spinning around and around and around. On his way to the bus, he took the rest of his acid. The trip home was better than usual. They almost hit an old man in a crosswalk.

He slammed the front door and stopped in the kitchen. "I want your ass here, now, this second!" It was his dad's voice. George strolled to the den, threw himself on the couch. Puff, their Siamese cat, got confused and leapt off. "What's this?" his dad bellowed, holding some paper up. It was Philippe's list.

George thought, "If I tell him the truth I'll have to sneak out from now on. But if I say it's a joke he'll think I'm crazy and then what?" He had to say something. "Someone I slept with once gave that to me. I thought it was weird, but she wants to be a biology teacher."

"What's the girl's name?" "Forget it! I'm not going to tell you that. She's just a strange girl. Besides, it's been months. Let's drop it." "No, this is serious, George," his dad shouted. "I know a little French. I've never seen such filth!" Phlegm flew out of his mouth when he got to the *f.*

George saw his chance to escape. "How dare you spit on me!" He rose to his feet. His dad shoved him back on the couch. "I'm taking you to see your mother," he said. "Maybe she can do something, I give up. Get your coat." George trotted into his room, swearing under his breath.

Drawers had been yanked out and dumped on the bed, posters ripped up, books thrown about. George was amazed by how flimsy his kingdom had been. One person had brought the thing tumbling down. Then he remembered his diary. He shoved his arm under the mattress. It was there, locked tight. "Phew!"

* * *

George was biting his nails when their car stopped in front of the hospital. "Can't I go see a psychiatrist instead?" he moaned. His dad shook his head. "Just go in. She's in room six thirty-nine, on the top floor. I'll be back in an hour." George entered the place thinking, "I'm not nearly stoned enough."

A nurse saw him traipsing around the halls. "You look like you're lost," she smiled. George admitted he was. The address plate for room six thirty-nine had apparently fallen off. She gave the door a push. "You're on your own." Inside, his mom was asleep. It looked permanent.

There was a video monitor near her head. A little light was drawing mountains across it. George watched for a while. It wasn't interesting. It was like one of those odd things that came on a TV screen after a station went off for the night. Was it trying to say something?

He listened to the mechanical whir of the monitor. Once he thought he heard a scratchy voice say, "This is it." "Oh!" Some nurse, a new one, had walked in. "You must be this woman's son. Just a minute, I'll wake her." Before George could say don't, she'd rustled her way to the bed.

She squeezed his mom's shoulder. Her eyes flipped open. She glanced around. "Your child's here," the nurse chirped. She left. George and his mother looked blankly at each other. "Hi. Dad dropped me off." She didn't say anything, so George peeked at the monitor. It held the same boring image.

By the time he got back to her face she was opening and closing her mouth. Finally sounds came out. "George," she sighed, then, after several more jaw movements, "yes." This was what George had expected. She'd become scary. He wanted some acid.

She was trying to talk again. "Your father," she wheezed, "told me . . . something." Her face scrambled in an attempt to remember. George couldn't think how to distract her. He smiled, hoping she'd tell him how cute he was. Eventually she did, not in so many words, but her eyes said it. Or he assumed they had.

He glanced out the window. All he could see was the wall of another wing. One of its windows was open and, though the insides were dark, he heard a TV set. That's where that voice must have come from. He couldn't tell what was on, maybe news or a soap opera. Something too serious.

"Nice day," he said. His mom appeared to agree. "So, school's going fine. You know me, I try . . ." He talked about every uninteresting thing he could think of. She watched him. At least her eyes were pointed his way. They could have been saying, "You're cute," or "It's a nice day," or "Go on."

He looked at the monitor. Its puny mountains were gone. There was a light jetting over the screen, a straight line being started again and again. It made him think of John, pencil to paper, erasing, redrawing, until he had gotten George right. When that thought disappeared, he saw the light.

He'd seen that happen in movies. He knew what it meant. He stared at his mom for a while. Then he stood up, walked into the hall and stopped the first nurse he saw. "Mom's . . . shit . . . dead." She yelled to another nurse, who came running. "Where?" they asked, kind of angrily. "The room with no number," George said.

He sat on a low brick wall near the hospital entrance. He watched people go in and out. As they approached the door it sensed their presence and swung open. There were doors like that everywhere, but he'd never thought about them before. He stood and inched toward it. When he was five feet away it opened.

The car drove up. George climbed in. They'd already gone a

few blocks when his dad asked, "How is she?" George thought a second. "Dead." He was glad when his dad didn't say anything. They made a U-turn, parked, locked up and walked toward the entrance. When they were five feet away from the door it opened.

"Well, it's over. She's dead. I don't know what I'm supposed to think. I just wish I hadn't been there when it happened. Dad thinks it's my fault. He didn't say so, but I can tell. Shit, he's the one who upset her. He did it, not me. I was just there.

"I'm going to use this to make myself change, like a starting point. I think that's the best thing to do. I won't buy any more drugs. I'll try not to do what I always do. I never do anything other than school and Philippe.

"Tomorrow I'll clean up my room and make it look like a normal place. I think I'll burn all my Disneyland stuff so I can't change my mind. Nobody else was ever interested in the stuff anyway and all my feelings for it are destroyed by the drugs now.

"I called Cliff tonight, just to talk. He doesn't care anymore. He kept saying how cute David was. I guess they're in love. He said that David is sort of obsessed or whatever with me. I don't know why, but it pisses him off. I hung up.

"It's strange I'm not sad about Mom. I guess it took such a long time I felt everything I could feel already. I wish I hadn't been there, but I'm glad the last person she looked at was me. She really loved me once. Likewise, I guess.

"I think I'm afraid of stuff. Maybe that's it. I was afraid Mom would die, but now she has and it's okay. I can't let it stop me from doing things. I'm going to keep that in mind from now on. I mean it.

"I'm not ready to sleep. I have one hit of acid left. I've

decided to take it and go visit Tom, Philippe's friend. It's like a party or something to say my goodbye to the person I am. I'll let you know what happens. I'm off."

George sat on a couch, sipping gin from a tumbler. Tom was building a fire in the fireplace. George was sufficiently high, but the way Tom was watching the flames made him jumpy. "So, whatcha been up to?" George asked. Tom jabbed a log with an iron bar. George tried again. "Nice place." He meant the paintings.

"A friend did them." Tom set down the bar. "My friend believes corpses dream," he said. "Try to imagine each work is the dream of a murdered child." George couldn't. "Poor baby. School hasn't done you a lick of good, has it?" George could relate to that. "Nope."

"But you don't need to know anything, do you? Your beauty is far more profound than the works of our fine intellectuals, don't you think?" "I don't know," George chortled nervously. "What a bizarre thing to say." Tom wandered over and kissed, or, rather, sucked George's mouth as if it were a snakebite.

George laughed so hard he spilled his drink on his shirt. Tom ripped it open. "Hey," George said, "I need to wear this tomorrow." "Don't kid me," Tom snapped. "You know you won't need a shirt." George didn't know what that meant, but he was too stoned to fight. "Okay, I'm sorry. Go on. Really."

George's new jeans got the same treatment. Next thing he knew everything he'd had on was turning black in the fireplace. Tom dragged him onto the rug, did the vacuuming bit on his ass. George tried to shit, but he just hadn't eaten enough. "That's okay," Tom said, and wiped his mouth. "I get the idea.

"Wait here." Tom left the room. George stretched his legs.

He'd begun to hallucinate slightly. He kept confusing the windows and paintings. "It's about time," he thought. Tom was a creep but now things wouldn't matter so much. He was about to go over and refill his tumbler when Tom came back.

"Lie on your stomach," he barked. George did. He heard a clinking noise, and felt a tiny sharp pain in his ass. "It's just some Novocaine," Tom muttered, "so I can take you apart, sans your pointless emotions." "That's considerate," George thought. Just then his ass grew so numb he felt sliced in half.

"Let's go." George, walking unsteadily, followed the man down a steep flight of stairs. Maybe it was the numbness but he couldn't see very well. There was something on one of the walls, a shelf? Things piled all over it? Tom took a piece of the blur in his hand. It looked fun. No, it looked kind of dangerous.

Tom raised the blur to the level of George's chest. "Do you know what's inside that cute body of yours?" George didn't have any idea, but he couldn't risk sounding naive. "I think I do." "Really?" Tom said. "You might be surprised. Would you like to know?" George shrugged. That seemed the safest response.

George was about to cry. He was right on the edge. He had to hand it to Tom. He couldn't remember the last time he'd been so upset. When Tom indicated the floor, George went flat. He heard a series of sounds. The only thing they remotely resembled was somebody chopping a tree down.

Tom didn't talk for a while. The sounds continued. George listened attentively. He realized he was being chopped down. He sort of wished he could know how it felt, but Tom was right. He'd be crying his eyes out and miss the good parts. It was enough to see his blood covering the floor like a magic rug.

The strange-sounding music stopped. George heard a soft voice. "Any last words?" it asked. George was surprised by the question. If he was supposed to be dead, how could he talk?

Still, why not? "Dead . . . men . . . tell . . . no . . . tales," he said in his best spooky voice.

When Tom didn't laugh George bit his lip. That's all it took. He burst into tears. He felt a couple of slashes across his back. "I said no fucking emotions!" Tom yelled. "Do you want me to kill you or not?" "No," George sobbed. "Well, then what are you doing here?" "I don't know," George blubbered, "I don't know."

He was rolled onto his back. Through his tears he saw Tom's glasses. "Get out of here!" They came flying off. "Now! Stand!" George struggled up to his feet. "I don't have anything to wear," he choked. Tom stormed out of the room, then came back with a blanket and threw it at George's head.

George made his way to the door. "No, this way," Tom said, forcing open a small window near the ceiling. "You'll drip all over my house!" George dragged himself through the dusty rectangle. A hand grabbed his ankle. "Don't tell anyone how this happened," Tom hissed. "You're dead if you do."

George stumbled home, crumpling to the sidewalk occasionally. When headlights appeared in the distance he hid in the closest bush. The walk took hours. The blanket was no help at all. It got soaked with blood and grew very cold. He'd cry awhile, then shiver, which made him cry again.

The house was dark. He climbed through his window. When he saw the ruins of his room it made him cry again. He found a note from his dad on the foot of the bed. "David called. Who's he?" "Good question," George thought, "and I've got a better one." He scrounged around in the rubble and found his mirror.

His ass wasn't really an ass anymore. He couldn't look at it. He dropped the mirror. It shattered. He walked down the hall and knocked twice on his dad's door. After a minute it opened. George looked in the man's puffy eyes. "Umm," he whispered, "I think you should call for an ambulance."

PHILIPPE

MAKE BELIEVE

Philippe, 43, was so drunk that the bones in his legs seemed to juggle each other. Every step entertained him, though progress was not in the offing. George used to laugh when the older man wobbled like this. To Philippe those were strange little comedies, maybe because they'd grown very infrequent.

He moved from the chair by the telephone to his bookshelf, which he leaned against, one palm outstretched across several spines. They were too slim to read and, at his pressure, receded into the dark at the back of a shelf, where he'd often considered installing a safe.

To keep from falling, he grabbed at the frame of an artwork, which held him upright but skidded sideways on its hidden wire, then tilted up at one end like a sinking steamliner, an image the picture resembled at times, though it was abstract.

"I like this," Philippe said, "because it is not in my way, but it makes the room change because it is not a burden, I think it is called, but is beautiful whatever I see in it. Now I perceive a sinking ship because I am drunk, and that is the best of all I have seen."

He laughed. "When I was in Paris," he thought. He could only remember one person, a boy named Jan who was Belgian and spoke in the strange French some Belgians used. Jan and he couldn't communicate, so they'd undressed. Jan was particularly, if not the best of the . . .

Philippe lost his balance. He clutched at some books, which came loose in his hand, and only managed to keep from collapsing entirely by gripping the arm of the chair with his other hand while waving the hand with the books until his knees could support his weight.

He pulled himself into the chair whose wooden arm had protected him. He looked around the room, which he could barely make out. The boy walked in. He was naked and still kind of damp from the shower. He stared at Philippe for a while, then shrugged and put on his clothes.

When he was dressed, the boy said, "I like you. You're strange, but you're nice." As he said this he gazed at the walls, not at Philippe. "You're from France," he added. Philippe was about to say where in France, but the boy started talking again. "Are you interested in me, because I could make an arrangement?"

Philippe didn't know if he was or not. "Come here," he said. The boy put his hands on his hips and walked over, then bent at the waist so his face was close enough to Philippe's to be studied, not kissed. "Men love me," he said, "because I'm reliable."

Philippe loved his face when it was indifferent, across a bar, but any expression at all hit his features as hard as an earth-quake. "I have someone," Philippe said, "but I know a man who will love you." He wrote down Tom's name and phone number.

"When is the best time to call him?" "Tomorrow or any-time," Philippe answered. The boy put the number somewhere on his person. He walked to the door, where Philippe couldn't see. "Oh, I'm Jimmy," he said. "Nice to meet you. Thanks."

Philippe checked his watch, then fell into a half-waking state for an hour, occasionally opening his eyes to double-check the room's tidiness. He needed this. When the buzzer rang he was a fraction more sober, and walked to the door with an obedient, almost refined sweep. "Yes, come in. How are you?" he asked.

George bolted past, found the chair he always used and sat down so hard its supports cracked. "Sorry. I'm, I don't know, fine," he mumbled. He drummed his fists on the arms. "It still hurts, but, you know . . . That's okay." Philippe shut the door, took a seat nearby. "You look tired," he said.

"What?" George asked. Philippe smiled reassuringly. George tried to. "No, I'm just nervous. I can't take acid now because that makes it throb, and I'm not used to being, you know, not stoned." Philippe asked if he wanted a drink. "It throbs," George repeated. His eyes became wooden.

Philippe stroked the boy's messy haircut. The scalp rubbed his palm in thanks. These gestures—the pressure from either side—felt as unusual to Philippe as the language he'd learned to pronounce. He wondered less what he meant by caressing than why he was wondering.

Regaining composure, he asked, "What, I mean how have you been?" George looked relieved. "Oh, I've been kind of

better," he said, then went into detail. Philippe could understand George since his English was simple. Still, it had a strange
current, circling around and beneath itself.

Philippe tuned in. ". . . My dad gave up, I guess. I think he
thought I'd change or something, and he's busy getting over my
mom, so as long as I'm there for dinner he doesn't care. It's kind
of bad, but he doesn't know where I am now. I try not to worry
about it, I mean what Tom did. I know it's my fault. . . ."

George continued, his lips nearly motionless. Philippe
smiled when a pause seemed to warrant warmth, knowing that
he could agree with whatever George said. The boy longed to
speak, and there was "nobody else to speak to," in his words,
which was some sort of privilege. Philippe felt removed from
these intervals.

"You sound good," Philippe said. George shut his eyes and
gripped the chair's arms. "Would you tell me something?" he
asked. "See, I have to make a decision. Umm, how do you feel
about me? I know you thought I was beautiful, and there's the
dead thing you do, but why?"

To Philippe's recollection, George hadn't probed before. Not
so much as "What day is it?" He peered at his glass for a
moment. "I think you are beautiful," he answered, knowing
those words were correct, "and I enjoy what we do." George bit
his lip. "You don't love me, right?"

"Yes," Philippe said. "I mean no, but I love what we do."
George's head dropped an inch. "I have to think about us," he
cringed, "because I'm not sure if we . . . Shit, wait a sec. It'll
pass." Philippe smiled, but that seemed inappropriate. He took
a drink.

Philippe watched George plod toward the rain-splattered street.
Once he tripped over a sprinkler head and fell flat on his face.

He struggled up, holding his elbow, and vanished behind a hedge. After a brief intermission, Philippe saw him wandering down the street with his thumb out.

He thought of opening the window to yell, "You are okay, Georges?" If he hadn't come with the boy a half hour ago, he might have splayed on the couch and rerun the best parts of this fall in slow motion. Instead he sealed the blinds, turned, and lowered his eyes to the spot where George usually lay.

The tumble enticed him since it was unreal. It was unreal since he hadn't observed the boy's face as he fell. When Philippe pictured George's expression approaching the ground, he saw pretend pain, the look that would creep over dolls' faces when children left them alone in the dark.

George was hurt, but the specifics could be imagined away. Philippe had repaired them, or given himself that impression, by making believe he'd messed up George himself. This cruelty, however imaginary, fell in line with his wishes. He'd focus his eyes on the new wear and tear and feel very complex.

When he looked at the scars he saw the inside of George, not as cold, gray and empty—as he preferred it to be—but brightly colored and very disorganized. On the negative side, they'd complicated his feelings for death by defining his view of it. On the positive side, they looked like fireworks.

Still, no matter how George had filled up with hieroglyphs, they didn't help Philippe figure things out. Scars merely forced him to stylize his thoughts, until the destruction he saw matched the painstaking beauty he knew in his mind's eye, his tinted lens.

He smiled and went into the kitchen, then dampened a few paper towels. He crouched on the living room rug, collecting the usual stray bits of shit, or, as he'd learned to describe them, "my smelling salts." That was a phrase used by mothers to indicate something that woke people up.

He downed a vodka, his ninth or tenth. When the phone rang he managed to answer it. Tom was calling to talk. He'd just killed someone new. They discussed that, then Tom asked, "How's George holding up?" Philippe considered the question. "Alive," he said.

This led Tom to deliver his typical speech. As Philippe understood it, the points were: (1) Tom realized that he shouldn't have done it, but (2) the worst mistake was in letting George live since (3) the boy knew too much, so (4) . . . Philippe changed the subject.

Philippe lay in bed imagining George's death. He was extremely drunk, his eyes were closed. The world he saw rang with percussion. Skeletons snapped. Blood and entrails exploded on a grand scale, while George, deposited deep in these fireworks, flailed like a tiny, crazed acrobat.

Philippe let himself have preposterous thoughts late at night. Sleepiness didn't discriminate. Death seemed a friend, being so far away. Everything else was a fairy tale. The only difference between, say, a pink unicorn and George's death was the chill off the mind that imagined the latter.

Still, this particular fantasy nagged him. He'd stroll through the streets, eat, bathe, weed his rose garden, and it would gather strength over his head, an insidious halo, as black as dried blood, glittering with the thunder of snapping bones.

It tugged at him like a tornado. He would peer up and see George affixed to its sphere, and the smog made him think of a woodcut he'd seen as a child. It showed every bone in some man's body broken and woven through spokes of a wagon wheel. Hoisted aloft in the Renaissance, they had continued to twirl for Philippe ever since.

This was the grave he'd handpicked for George. It spiraled into the darkness tonight, like a piece of cheap dinnerware covered with jewels, thrown away by a terrified man to re-create the impression of UFOs, or the unknown at least, in the trickier glow of his thoughts.

The UFO reached an ambiguous distance. Philippe changed it into a wound. He was looking inside George's body itself, seeing the tiniest thread of its jumble, the way one might study a theater set if the actual play was impenetrable or performed in a foreign language.

He thought of a huge, torn-up asshole. It belonged to a boy named Ed. That was before George came into the picture. Ed was unbearably cute, until men had worn him away. They'd fastened him to a treadmill that spun until there was nothing around but a vague outline, smeared with blood.

Philippe used to say, "I am going to kill this Ed." He'd meant that. At the moment, he simply pronounced the words, disregarding their meaning, as though he were saying, "Please don't," to the jaws of a lion. A death was beyond his means. He could only squint blearily into its depths, the casual bystander.

When he did, he saw a set of teeth, shiny as jewels, puzzled together and hung from invisible wires. It suggested the bones of a frail human body, and gave off an eerie if elegant glow like a chandelier, though hung so low it blew wildly about in his heated breaths.

He lit a cigarette. The bed was soaked with sweat. When he let his mind drift like this, it beautified every idea he had, but while this rendered them livable, their newfound brilliance left sleep's entrance so shadowy . . . "Quick," he thought, "think straight."

*   *   *

Two years ago Philippe had moved to America. He found its dingiest bars. He paid a series of hustlers to lie very still on his floor and gained a wild reputation. One of his fucks introduced him to someone who then introduced him to someone who'd started a club for men with unusual tastes.

Philippe became the ninth member. They'd meet at the ringleader's house every couple of weeks. Each participant wanted to kill someone cute during sex. None had summoned the strength, so they'd formed a committee to solve the problem of their weakness.

Ed was the evidence. One of the members had found him in some hole. His ass had no muscle tone whatsoever. It billowed out from his back and was always as cold as ice cream. He'd stumble over. They'd act out scenarios using him as a prop, then he'd lurch off.

Philippe found relative peace through this teamwork. It brought certain haunting ideas into focus, particularly shit. It was their major find. It formed a kind of stumbling block, in one's words, between them and their wish. It was, in another's terms, death's mace.

In time, their discussions grew more and more abstract, with references to theological theories and artists' renditions. They lost Philippe, whose grasp of English was basic at best. When even Ed became history, Philippe thought of driving an ambulance.

One night a member asked if he could bring someone in to do a film presentation. The vote was unanimous. The man had a backlog of deaths in the can, as he phrased it. He set up equipment and laid out some background. "The boy you're about to see hitchhiked . . ."

He'd picked up the hitchhiker, coerced him home, got him drunk, numbed his body with Novocaine, led him into a basement, started the film rolling, mutilated his ass, asked if he'd like to say any last words, to which the boy had said, "Please don't." Then he'd killed him.

The only sound in the room was the clicking projector. Sometimes the clicks and stabs matched for a few seconds. That made the whole thing seem fake. Then the boy made a very bland face. "Is he dead?" someone asked. "No," the man answered. "Not yet. Watch."

Philippe was astonished. He found himself drifting away, as one tended to do with pornography, or, rather, drifting into the image itself, like a child did when watching cartoons. He'd knelt down a short distance away from them, too shy to join in.

His memory fragmented the rest. Philippe could remember hands scooping out bloody intestines. At what seemed a hap-hazard point, everyone in the room heard a brief, curt an-nouncement. "Now," it said. Philippe knew that word, but he hadn't realized what it meant at first.

The film ended. It flapped like a bat. People redid their pants. The place felt cold, just a vague square of yellowish light. It shone on their sweaty faces. The man switched it off, flicked a switch on the wall. On came the table lamps.

"What are you feeling, Philippe?" Tired. "Then you should sleep." But I am too tense; I keep thinking. "What kind of thinking?" Well, everything. "Of Georges?" Some. He repre-sents something I have desired for a long time. "How long?" Since before I came to America.

"Why did you come?" I came because in my own country I felt afraid. "Of what?" Everything, but mainly of myself. I was beginning to want what I could not have. "Can you be more clear?" No. When I try, my beliefs or desires come out beautiful. They *are* beautiful to me, but I cannot understand them in that form.

"You wanted to kill someone?" That is too simple. I thought about killing someone, though I did not know who. My ideas about death are very beautiful, so I wanted to think about killing a beautiful person. "A boy?" Yes. "And you could not find him there?" I could not find myself there. I was known as what I am not.

"Who are you?" I am trying to find this out. It is hard. I am driven to do certain things, and I believe they are helping me, because they seem strong. "Why Georges?" He makes me feel something. I do not know this answer. "He has been hurt?" Yes. "By someone you know?" Yes.

"How would you kill Georges?" Very slowly, so I could see everything in him and know what he has meant to me. "Would you expect to see yourself in him?" I would expect to see someone who could answer my questions looking at me through him. He would resemble me.

"And Tom?" He is me if I were less alone. "Can you explain that?" He can kill someone, because he knows who he is. He kills someone to make a friend, I think. To know someone else. I would kill, if I could do that, to know myself. We are different, but I understand him.

"Why did you share Georges with Tom?" To compare myself to him. "Have you learned something?" I have seen small differences, but they are hard to explain. I think he felt hatred for Georges in his hurry to find a friend. I feel something like love for Georges, though I do not know why. "Are you weak?" Yes. "Would you like to change that?" I would not know how.

"Have you made progress?" I am beginning to feel there is no answer for me. I am too interested in what is beautiful, and when beauty is not somewhere, I create it. But when something is beautiful it is impossible for me to understand. "How do you mean this?" I mean beauty is powerful. I feel very weak when I see it, or when I create it. No, I cannot explain.

"Death is beautiful?" It is too beautiful to explain. "But you try." I must. "Why?" Because I must know what I love, because it is me. "I do not understand." I do not either. "You wish to die?" No, I wish never to die, but to see myself in death. To know what I am in the answer of death. I am becoming completely lost. Help.

"I do not know how." You should tell me why I do these things. "But I cannot, you know this." Yes. "So what will you do now?" I think I must sleep and try to forget about everything. "Do you think you will do this?" No, but I must, and I am nearly asleep.

STEVE

THE FOREFRONT

One month ago I decided to use our garage for a nightclub. I told Dad the yard was so huge that my noise wouldn't bother the neighbors, and how out of touch he'd grown. He agreed. I felt sure he would. I can't remember the last time he turned me down. It's a four-car garage with this peaked ceiling, criss-crossed by sturdy oak beams that make me think of a church, though I've never been in one. It didn't need much alteration. I just moved stuff out into the storeroom and painted the walls flat black. I like flat black. It doesn't try to explain anything, and it's been hip since before I was born, I guess.

Tonight's the opening. I Xeroxed flyers and put one in every locker at school. I knocked a hole in the wall, which will act as an entrance. My oldest friend, Keith, made some music tapes. He'll man the sound on this platform we laid across part of the rafters. Fred and Jerry from gym class agreed to be bouncers. Another friend, Jane, will tend bar. To the left of the bar are two portable toilets Keith found on a freeway construction site. One is for pissing and shitting. The other's my office, so called. That's where I plan to seduce people, as well as do what real club owners must. I think of everything.

My club's called The Forefront. That's the name of a band I like. They're obscure so most people will guess it's original. A while ago Mom and Dad popped in to check out the premises. He strolled around and went, "Hmm," when things caught his eye. Keith said that meant he was tongue-tied. Mom's worried some drunk will scratch her car, which is parked on the street. I reassured her, then thought, "Yeah, she's probably right." They just left. I'm crazy about the club's door. It's so raw. You can see all the plaster and everything. It looks like someone wanted in so intensely they couldn't wait.

When I tell Keith I'm off to the shower, he doesn't hear. Then I notice the headphones. I point toward the house, he points at the tapedeck, I flip him off, he gives the okay sign, I laugh, he laughs. Well, if nothing else happens tonight I'll take him up on his offer. He has a dazzling ass, though I'm bored with it. I can't remember the night we met. It was two years ago when we were sixteen, I guess. I was drunk. He looked exactly like somebody else. He still does, but nowadays when we fuck I can guess what he's thinking. That doesn't ruin the experience. On the other hand, it doesn't help.

The shower head has a massage unit. It makes my skin itch, but tilted up slightly and aimed at one wall, the stall roars like a fountain. I sprawl near the drain and peer up at the steam, which

I use like a horny kid uses his pillow. It's Keith. I use Keith as a
model because I can draw mental pictures of him. After a while
I stop dreaming it's him, hide his face with some strangers' until
I arrive at this star from the sixties who played John Wayne's son
in *In Harm's Way*. I make his eyes look in love with me. I moan,
that echoes. I spurt on my chest. I should've waited until
tonight.

I towel off, then slip into my suit. It cost Dad a fortune. The
coat and pants are made out of this light fabric, dark gray with
black smears and white crinkly lines. They look like cigarette
ashes. My shoes come to sharp points. They used to be brown
but I painted them white so my feet would seem bigger. My hair
stands on end, thanks to Tenax. If I didn't know my reflection
I'd fuck me to death. I'm sort of ogling it when my mom
appears over its shoulder. "I'm worried your music will keep us
awake," she says. How many times have I told them their
bedroom's so far away from the garage, all they'll hear is a very
low, regular thump? "It'll lull you to sleep."

Back in the club Jane is stacking up beer cans behind the bar,
which is really an ironing board spray-painted red. It's supposed
to look stupid. Fred and Jerry are giving her shit, but it's all just
a mating dance. Mostly it shows up as awkwardness, which, on
guys their height and build, means a very broad slapstick.
"Ahem," I say. They scurry over. "Stand guard, and if anyone
tries to sneak in who isn't dressed like they live in the
mid-1980s, send for me." They answer, "Right," simul-
taneously. Fred's cute. I'd sit on his face, if he shaved first.

Keith starts his soundtrack. We've a mutual fondness for
gloomy perspectives and danceable beats. When they clash, it
creates the impression our bodies are headed somewhere, not
just losing weight. That's the finishing touch. Our garage disappears in the tar-colored paint. Any second now people will file

in with better-than-average looks on their faces. I take a cruise through the room. When nobody is watching—and who would?—I lean down and kiss the cement, my way of christening the place. "Make me famous," I say in a jokey voice. Keith saw me do it. He's licking his tapedeck. "Eat shit!"

Here they come. I shake hands with the first several entrants, then climb up the ladder and sit beside Keith. He lays out four lines of his private cocaine on the tapedeck. We snort it away through a ten-dollar bill. As the room starts to bustle we chat in a nerve-wracking whine we've developed to crack ourselves up. A great new song by The Swans is drowning us out. "Greed," I think it's called. We go insane when this born-again Christian we know actually sobs when the lyrics begin. "Carl, they're *ironic!*" That's hilarious, at least on coke. Coke also makes Keith seem different, by which I mean better, by which I mean hot.

"Steve!" It's Jerry. He waves his arms wildly, then heads for the door. I descend from the platform, salute a few friends and rearrange my suit. Just as I'd hoped this shambling boy a little cuter than me has appeared in his usual posthippie, prepunk regalia: old jeans, frayed T-shirt, unkempt hair. He's decayed of late, but it works. "Boss," Fred says firmly, "I thought we'd consult you on this." The boy—his first name's on the tip of my tongue—looks very drunk and collapsible. "Yes, I can see what you mean," I sigh, wagging my head. "Young man, please come to my office."

I lock us inside and sit down on the seat cover. He stands between me and the door, trying to keep his eyes open. "We've got a problem here," I announce, using my dad's tone of voice. He doesn't say anything. "Look, I'm going to say something ugly. Since this is my club, and you obviously don't like its rules, why should I treat you respectfully? I'll let you stay, for a price." I suppose that strange frown on his face means his wallet is empty. "No, my club, your ass." It's a terrible line but I had to think fast. "Okay?" He frowns at me for a while, then slowly nods his head. I follow him out.

The club's a humongous hit. I waste my time on Keith's perch, mouthing lyrics and bragging about my success with—I still don't remember his name. Keith wants a rundown first thing in the morning. It's late. A few dancers keep bouncing around, but the sidelines are empty except for a few tangled couples and wallflowers. My flower's wilted. He's flat on the floor. If he'd tried to leave, I gave my bouncers permission to get in the way. I can't remember the pretext. "Keith, can you lock up?" "Asshole," he snarls, which I guess means he will. I climb down the ladder. The boy sees me coming, I think.

I don't know what to say. We're in bed. George has passed out or gone to sleep. His ass looks like somebody threw a grenade at it. He said he fell on some glass. I covered it with a blanket as soon as he dozed off. I tried to seem interested. I closed my eyes and formed a picture of Keith. Even then, when I started to finger-fuck George, which is my favorite sex act, I might as well have been trying to plug a leak. He just lay there and let it go on, as if I were a bad dream or something. I almost threw up twice. At one point I paused and sort of shook him, but he'd faded into wherever he is at the moment.

Normally when I'm in bed with someone I'm not hot for I ask him to leave. I wish I'd said so the second George stripped. If I kick him out now, I'll feel guilty forever. I'd always worry I might have helped, not that I know how I could. He must get rejected a lot. I mean, his face is so promising. I could phone at least four friends tomorrow and break their hearts, plus put myself in a privileged position. His ass *is* a great piece of gossip. So why am I looking at him like my dad looked at me when I fell off our roof? Is that love, or anywhere close to it?

I don't understand the word, though I've relied on it often enough. Saying "love" is like yelling "Ouch!" when something should hurt but doesn't. It's a quick way to win points. For instance, last weekend I slept with a tall, gloomy boy in an overcoat. He was at Music Plus buying the same British import I had. I coaxed him home. We didn't smile at each other once. Sex was defined by our musical tastes. We fooled around with our crotches and assholes like they were knobs on a stereo amp. I decided "I love you" would sound good against a shrill background. It did. I wish I had it on videotape.

The closest I've come to saying something like that with sincerity was to an older guy. He had this trick where he'd say, "Spill your guts." While I did, he would nod his approval as if I were reading his mind in the right tone of voice. He had me fooled. I said I loved him so often he ran out of clever retorts. The tenth time you hear it, "Oh, Steve, you're too kind" isn't sweet anymore. The last time we met I was searching for him in the glare on a windshield. All I saw were his fists. They were hooked on the steering wheel. The rest seemed, and still is, shit.

The way I feel about George is a first. Wait, I take that back. When I was twelve I hung around with a gang of boys who, like myself, were obsessed with—I hate to admit it—Led Zeppelin. One guy's younger brother was dying to join us. He'd sit down nearby wearing very bright clothes so we couldn't not notice him. After a while I decided I had more to gain from the boy than from knowing who'd played lead guitar on which album. I waved. He waved back. I think he was cute and had a slight speech impediment. Two days or so later I heard a noise at my parents' front door.

We'd meet on the weekends, see movies. His eyes had big question marks scribbled all over them, like a character in a comic book. "What's going on?" he'd ask, and I'd fill him in— "When couples like one another they scream a lot," for example. Then the word "gay" snuck into the dialogue of some movie. When my friends dreamt of X-raying skirts, I'd been bored, or felt antsy at best. But boys' pants were still seat covers, grass-stained and worn loose on purpose. "Gay is what David Bowie pretends to be when he makes records." Weeks passed. We were looking through one of my mom's fashion magazines. I'd paused too long on this picture: a woman in topless bikini, her back to the camera.

"She looks like me," my friend gasped. He was eyeing the image with what I guess is called wonder. "How so?" I asked. "I don't know," he replied. That was my cue to explain the world. I examined the girl's back again. Meanwhile he removed his shirt and stood facing the window. I glanced from one to the other. I guess it was only the pose, but I wanted his body and, as with the girl in the photograph, I didn't know how to reach it nor what I would do if I could. So I held back, did nothing. He died in a plane crash soon after. I must have the clipping somewhere. I loved him. I think I could say that, if someone were listening.

The sun's up. I want to tell George what I'm thinking about. But it takes me a while to actually reach out my hand, maybe ten minutes. "George?" His eyes open. I say where he is, how terrific last night was, how much I enjoy what I know of him, the desire to be friends or more than friends, that he's special, I know this already, and so on. He doesn't answer. I hear myself mouthing stuff I can't believe, yet I want him to think I'm not lying, he means something, who knows what, I can't describe it, believe me. He smiles at that, which I will take to mean "Thanks."

Now I'd like him to leave, temporarily anyway. I want to put on a record and rethink my night, get the messy or half-baked ideas out. I set a date when we'll meet again. He takes the hint, hits his feet, and looks around for his shorts. In the daylight his scars are more savage. If I had to compare them to anything, I'd say a human brain drawn by a four-year-old. I want to see it in friendly terms, so we can joke about it at some point. But not now. I really feel like I'm going to faint if he doesn't . . . I notice his shorts lying under my desk chair. "There they are," I shriek, "there . . . *there.*"

I just woke up from a dream, the kind where you recognize where you are and how you're acting, but not why or what it means. It made me think of some underground films I've watched, so cheaply made you can feel the director's hands, and see the actors as well as the characters, but too poetic to follow. I was raking leaves in our front yard. Each time I'd lift my rake, the leaves would return to their places. I knelt down, looked closely. The fuckers were painted. The lawn was a huge cloth stretched over the ground. Just then everything grew very dark, like it's supposed to do during an eclipse. I glanced up. I was inside my club.

I felt nervous. The Forefront looked different, its bar lit by banks of lights, ripped velvet couches along the walls and, most unnerving, the entrance seemed very meticulous. I'd tried too hard to simulate rawness. It felt calculated and chic, which are my least favorite feelings on earth. I searched around for a hammer, intending to smash things. That took forever. A crowd began forming outside, their faces pinched with impatience. I glanced at my watch. The club was supposed to be open, but none of my friends had shown up to work.

I knew I should calm the crowd down, but when I looked out again, they were no more lifelike than the leaves at my feet. Someone had walled up the hole and drawn a crowd on the plaster. Amazed, I walked toward it. The drawing grew vaguer, first impressionistic, then clouded, its surface illusory like marble. Soon I began to see patterns. The swirls became streaks that connected like lines on a road map. The lines became cracks. They sprouted tinier ones. I tried to run. The wall, the club, the garage collapsed.

I'd pulled the blankets over my head. Which came first, the afterimage of light through woven cloth, or the dream wall? Did I wake up before, hide my head, then return to sleep? It doesn't matter. I'm startled, though not so upset I can't shampoo my hair. I drift through breakfast, then drift through the first half of school. I'm a minor celebrity, thanks to the club. Two weeks after the opening, students still yell, "You're . . . that guy," or "Can't wait to get back to The Forefront again."

In twenty-eight minutes and thirteen seconds the lunch bell will ring. I've agreed to meet up with a guy named John something, who wants to propose a mingling of the club with his artworks. Until then I'm foraging through my bad dream, seeking symbols and so forth, because of this ancient book we've been discussing in English class. It seems that in B.C. years, dreams were considered advisory. Governments, armies, religious types used them as maps to their destinies. So far I think that mysterious wall implied George. Everything else seems peripheral, though I admit I'm afflicted with love's tunnel vision at present.

There's John by the half-dead magnolia tree. Each time he gets the same haircut it's more dated. I used to think he was cute. He had a big show of drawings at school a few months ago. I agree with Keith. He looked them over and quipped, "Here's a

guy who'd watch newsreels of Nazi death camps, then say
something like, 'Wow, this old black-and-white film stock is
beautiful.' " The only reason I'm talking to him is his boyfriend, who's scrumptious but nowhere in sight. We shake
hands. He makes his proposal. The plan is to do a theme night,
hang his portraits around and have a reading of poems by this
closet case teacher McGough, his co-conspirator.

Sounds good. I'm all for creating an atmosphere to keep my
patrons on edge. Besides, George has a birthday this weekend.
I'll dedicate it to our love or, better yet, make the night a
surprise party thrown in his honor. "Okay," I grin. Once the
date's fixed, we sit and just stare at each other. With him, it's my
natural tendency anyway. There's something generic about his
face, like it belongs on a bust titled *Man*. I think what I wanted
to fuck about him was his makeup. Toned down, he's a mild
shock at best. "Here," he says suddenly, "this will explain it."
He hands me a folder and walks away.

I take a leisurely scan through the contents. First there's a
handful of poems, which I'll scrutinize later. On first glance
they seem overwritten. The Xeroxed pages of John's art are
more my speed. They're dark and messy on purpose, I'm sure.
A scribbled note says they're part of a series called "Owner-
ship," that one and two should be paired off. Three and four,
five and six, likewise. Each duo contains an incompetent face
(left), and a primitive ass (right). I think they portray real-life
couples. I guess the idea is all asses are very alike and their
value depends on the people who love them or something. Page
five looks familiar. I hold it at arm's length, squint. Sure
enough, John's in there somewhere, which must mean the tur-
moil on page six is what's-his-name's ass. I turn it this way, then
that, hold it up to the light.

I squeal into our driveway and tiptoe upstairs before Mom

says, "Nice day, Steve?" Reaching my bed, I collapse and unzip my slacks. The drawing clenched in my left fist, I zoom past the pencil marks, mentally discarding each clumsy, extraneous line until John's lover's ass is my property. I need immense concentration to sort it out, and, even then, the thing's pretty shapeless, like spilled milk. I'm so involved I mistake a loud knock on my door for the sound of my heart. "Uh, Steve?" It's George's voice. That's right, we agreed he'd drop by today. I shove my cock down my pants, hide the drawing and let him in.

When I see his face I think, "Why not have sex right this second, while what's-his-name's ass is still fresh?" I kiss him brusquely. He tastes like a hamburger. I steer us onto the bed. Clothes are flying around. He lies on his back. I fold his legs until his knees touch his shoulders. I pin them there with my shoulders. There are almost identical spots on each ass-cheek where his skin's as smooth as a normal boy's. I press my hands down there, stick my cock up his ass, then look into his eyes. They seem scared of the ceiling for some reason. I can't believe my luck. He's very loose, but I find if I press very hard he tightens up, and there's enough inner friction to get me off.

Afterward we sit and talk. As usual, I'm the big blabbermouth trying to suss out what he has been doing. "Nothing," is his final word on the subject. Okay, I won't press. Instead I play an old Sisters of Mercy LP. I like them because they're so stoned or depressed or whatever, they think their own deaths are a hip place to be. I'm content on the outskirts, one eye on how George is reacting. He's facedown a few feet away, lying so still it's like he's not listening, more like he's dead or has left his nude body idling in my room. It's a spooky sight. I'm almost sure I'm in love with it.

*   *   *

One hour and counting. Keith's on his perch cueing tapes with a coked-out expression. John's hanging the last of his portraits. They cover the walls. His boyfriend is striking ridiculous poses behind a microphone stand, where McGough will deliver some poetry I never read. He's in my office, rehearsing his stuff. Fred and Jerry just told me John's drawings are "sick." Jane's her same old reliable self, stacking beer cartons, penciling signs which read, "Please tip." I've positioned myself dead center, ringmaster-like, and conduct them with jabs and shouts.

I'm tense. See, I hadn't told John that tonight was a party until a few minutes ago. When George's name came up, he swore and stormed off. McGough explained that to me. George and John were an item. He found it amusing. Now I'm worried about *his* connection, because he hazed over at one point, clapped his hands and said, "Miles here? Terrific!" I guess I could take down the banner which reads "The George Miles Club," or is that too drastic? There could be a thousand more items out there in the world. I'm a latecomer. Accept it, jerk.

I try to relax by watching John's friend pretend he's whoever. George Michael? He looks like a twerp, or I use this excuse to slow him down for a chat. "Getting ready for later on?" I suggest. He quits moving mechanically, smiles at me, blushes. "Yes, I am." We start to talk about nothing much. Unlike most pretty boys, he doesn't seem to be letting his looks do the work, merely speaking through them with an anomalous voice, like someone at a costume ball. It's disconcerting, as though I'm addressing him, then being answered by an interpreter. We're out of things to say, shake hands. I let myself hold his a second too long. Who knows what message he's getting?

I stroll down a row of John's drawings. Some of the models are still recognizable, people I've seen around school. Then I notice the tags. These aren't couples, but different parts of the same person. I think of that scene on my bed with the sketch in my fist. I glance back at the kid, who's conferring with John, about me, I guess. "Hey," yells the artist. He glides over. "My little friend thinks you're cute. I mean he thinks George is cute, but he likes George's men. Look, I'll explain it some other time. Point is, you interested? Sex, I mean. Now, him."

I'm torn. "Sure," I say, "but I don't even know the guy's name." "David," John smiles, "like the statue." He rejoins the beauty. He puts his hand over the microphone, says a few words, pats David's head and nudges him in my general direction. David's gorgeous. He's smiling like people do under hypnosis. It's pointed here, but I don't feel the warmth. I nod. He nods. I walk, assuming he'll follow. I peer up at Keith. His eyes are moving with us through the room. When he's sure it's the office we're aimed at, his fist hammers down on the tapedeck.

I'm poised to knock on the door when I'm sideswiped by John again. "Steve," he gasps, "do you know Cliff?" I shake my head. "If you meet him tonight"—then he whispers so David can't hear—"don't mention this." Whoosh. He's somewhere across the club. What's that about? I knock gently. McGough sticks his head out. I don't have to ask. He grabs a handful of papers and leaves, mumbling something too flowery to be intended for us. We're in. I could ask what the George angle is but that'd waste time and force me to question my motives. Instead I strip him while he shifts his weight from one leg to the other.

Our choices are standing or taking turns on the toilet. I hog the latter. He revolves jerkily, feeding me parts of his front and back. He's very clean and kind of tasteless, like plastic. I try the old finger approach, really scrounge around inside his ass. Even there, where I'd expect some surprises, he's smooth and immaculate. My first impression returns, that his beauty and he are in different worlds, with separate aims. Only now it's his skin I've engaged and he's elsewhere. Once he looks down and includes me in some unknown way in his thoughts. Another time he says something I can't really hear in a strange voice.

"Face the door, okay?" Asses are peaceful. I like them the same way I like flat black paint, and his is one of the flattest I've seen. George's must have resembled it. Not long ago I went to bed with a guy who was wild about mine. He drew a smile-face on it with a grease pencil, to justify his desires, I guess. But it's the plainness that gives me these goose bumps. I pry the cap off a Vaseline jar, coat one fingertip, wipe it off inside his ass, screw him onto my cock. He bounces up and down. I kiss his shoulders and shoot. "Was I a hit?" he asks, freeing himself. "Sure, great," I say, zipping up. "Tell George I'm great, okay?" I say I will, but I won't.

He turns left (John), and I turn right (entrance). People are filing through. Keith's tape has reached a song so obscure even I can't recognize who's singing. This one deserves its obscurity, but the funereal pace strikes the right tone and nobody's listening anyway. Suddenly Fred, asked to signal when George hits the foot of the driveway, waves his arms. I take my place at the microphone, tap to make sure it's on and say, "Ladies and gentlemen, as you may already know, tonight's a surprise party. The guest of honor will walk through the door any second. When I count to three, raise your beers and shout, 'Our hero!' "

Heads swivel around. People furthest back stand on their toes. My view is blocked. I hear George's voice squeak, "Oh, shit." I forget to count. Keith must have noticed me frozen in place. He shouts, "One-two-three!" Bottles soar, voices clash, yet the message is clear. I weave through the drunks to the first strains of Keith's pretaped greeting, "The Theme from *2001*." When I reach George he's trembling, as he occasionally does. "It's okay," I say. "Nobody's looking at you anymore."

George is so stoned he can't fix his eyes on me. "Steve?" he slurs. "Who're they?" I explain how tonight is a gift from the good part of me, the part of me who means well and couldn't hurt him. He's smiling. I'm going to say it. I haven't meant it since I was three or whatever. "I love you, George." I think I meant that. I think he heard, though interpreting someone's expression is hardly a science, at least for me. I tend to guess. My guess is he's too scarred to think about love at this time, but may later, which is the most anyone can expect.

We watch McGough read. People keep entering the club, so there's a continual din at the door. McGough will say something too fancy and incomprehensible, then we'll hear, "Hey, what the fuck's going on?" The only reason he's not being pelted with beer is the teacher mystique. A few braver students have slunk away, including David. He's back by the wall being George Michael. Not sexy. I put my arm around George. He rests his chin on my shoulder. I kiss his temple, believe it or not. That's when I hear this roar. It's growing louder. I can't hear the poetry anymore. I turn and look. David's playing an air guitar. He strikes an especially violent chord.

A car smashes right through the wall, rolls over David and comes to rest, barely scratched, in a heap of bricks. The driver's and passenger's doors open. Two guys with long hair step out holding half-empty bottles of vodka. They fall down. They roll around laughing and banging their fists on the floor. The passenger gets to his feet, but is too out of it and collapses, laughing. The driver catches his breath long enough to squeal, "Sorry we're late." That makes them howl again. I step over the passenger, crouch and peer under the wreck.

David's body is shredded like paper. His insides have pushed through some holes in his shirt, blue and greasy and jumbled. It looks like a flower bed. I have to imagine he's something else or I'll throw up. "Get help!" I yell. The passenger has risen up on his elbows. He's taking a drink from the bottle. Where's George? McGough knocks some people aside and asks, "Is he dead?" I nod. He leaves, then I hear his amplified voice say, "I want to ask you, please, for a minute of silence." *Where's George?* When things quiet down I hear the driver still laughing. I walk around the front end of the car and kick him as hard as I can in the head.

So much for The Forefront. Police came. After arresting the longhairs and making sure David's corpse got to the ambulance, they said our house wasn't zoned for a nightclub. I shut down. Dad hired some workers to fix the walls. It's a four-car garage again. I'm still upset about that. Two days ago this freckled guy in a wheelchair, whose parents are richer than mine even, offered to have his dad, a politician of some sort, bribe the police if I made him co-owner and renamed the place Haunted Nightclub. I gave that one-tenth of a second's thought. By far the best thing to come from the accident is George's ass, which doesn't frighten me now. I can look at it, like you can look at a horror film.

It's like this: I think I was after perfection, but wouldn't admit it. Take my weird dream where the club was transformed from a ratty hole into a fake ratty hole, and the tensions between the two caused my whole dream to collapse. I had this dualistic thing going on in my head, loving George—a mess—and wanting David—a perfect mess. I was a lot more confused than I let on. This sounds crazy, I know, but when I saw David there with his insides exposed, the perfection thing uglified. Is that a word? I mean, perfection's like God. It only works if you want it to badly enough, or . . . Shit, I'm all tangled up.

I'll try again. I could have used David's death as an excuse to believe in perfection, since I'd never gotten to know him aside . from his looks, so, in a sense, being dead, he *is* perfect. I went to his funeral. It crossed my mind. There's a kind of excitement about any box when you don't feel you know what's inside. It was like Christmas in hell, standing there with those other friends, hearing a priest tell us David would live in our hearts forever. Then they buried the thing, so none of us would feel left out I guess. "We all suffer," he said. The box made a terrible creak as it went under.

When that was over the kid's mother, a total drunk I might add, came up to George and asked, "Are you George?" He told her he was. "Well," she said, "David talked about you all the time. It was hard for his father and me to separate what he fantasized—which was a lot, if truth be told—from his real life. But now I see you are real and I know you two must have been special friends, so let me thank you for taking good care of our boy, for Dave, his dad, and myself." She left. George shot me one of his terrified looks. "I said maybe ten words to him in my whole life," he whispered. "The guy was insane. I never liked him for one minute."

He sat down so suddenly I almost tripped over him. Then, with the ominous voice of what I think are called mediums, like at séances, he told me exactly what happened to him that he came to be "like this." He didn't remember that much—I sat down—because he'd been stoned, and his manner of speaking leaves everything sketchy, so it was a chore to keep names, dates, et cetera, straight, but the story was scary enough that I flopped on my back at one point, sort of theatrically, though I couldn't have helped it, and felt like crying, except I don't cry. I never do. It just absolutely never happens.

It's four days later. I'm telling Keith how I phoned the old man who hurt George and announced if he ever got anywhere near us, that if anyone in my small circle of friends or acquaintances disappeared, I'd call the cops. He could do what he wanted but not in my world. I didn't say who I was, and hung up. Keith is shaking his head. We're in bed. We just had sex, which was very expected and pleasant. "I'm sure it's true," he says. "Trouble is, I only know about death from song lyrics and movies, so I don't know how to react, except to say, 'Wow,' though it's a bigger, more serious 'Wow' than usual."

We decide to have sex again. As we do, I take occasional snorts from Keith's cocaine supply. Coke creates distances between its users and others, especially other users. That's how Keith can be my oldest friend one minute, a relative stranger the next. Even without coke that happens. I think it's the voice. People don't really know one another except when they're speaking. As soon as they shut up, no matter how close they've been, that understanding is gone. They become cute, ugly, tall, short, fat, thin. I find this frightening most of the time, but it's the best part of sex. Keith's just some hot guy I picked up. Nice.

Afterward he hands me most of his coke. "For George," he says, "who deserves it." He claims he'll call me tomorrow. He has an idea we could restart the club. He knows of this old house that nobody lives in, not far from here. According to him, we could fix up its living room, soundproof the walls and continue in privacy, by invitation. I guess it's possible. ". . . Speaking of which, I've been dying to tell you a secret," he grins, "but promise you'll keep it quiet." My eyes widen. He rolls his. "I'm seeing John." He opens his wallet, then slides out some paper. He unfolds the paper and shows me. It's a terrible drawing, of Keith, I guess. "That's just a Xerox," he says, "but the original's some kind of masterpiece."

I'm surprised. Keith's great, but facially he's not in David's league, and, according to what I know, John isn't really Keith's type. Keith's a perfectionist, same as I was. I congratulate him and we have a brief talk about whether we've grown more mature or not. He's gone. I sit around for a while, then I follow the sound of the TV set into our den and join my mom on the couch. Dad's in the bathroom, apparently. "What's this?" I ask. "An extremely intelligent drama," she says, and recounts the award-winning life of its main star, an ancient woman whose name has the word *Dame* in front of it. I get involved in the show because the Dame's grandson character, who sits at a table and doesn't say anything, is my age and cute.

It must be four hours long, yet the boy stays peripheral, appearing once in a while to remind us, I guess, of how old the old woman is. When George rings our doorbell I don't care if things work out. We head to my room and sit around. It's hard to know how to say what I feel because (1) I've never paid much attention, and (2) George never answers me anyway. "Look what Keith gave us," I smirk, producing the coke. We do some, which makes him look different. He lies on the bed and unbuttons his shirt. Great nipples. I cross the room, switch off the lights and try to feel my way to him again. "George?" I just hit my leg on a table or something. It's really black in here.